In Young Adult fiction, voice is everything. *Ship in the Sky* brings it! With a gritty yet lyrical and singular voice, *Ship in the Sky* creates an in-depth world that at times evokes apocalyptic literature like McCarthy's *The Road* in tone. It's an adventure, to be sure, but more importantly, a journey, which is not the same thing.

The story celebrates perseverance and relationships between human beings (and a great dog!) that will satisfy readers looking for connection from their stories and characters.

—Tom Leeven, author of *Hellworld, Heartless,* and *Can't Wait for Tomorrow*

Ship in the Sky taps into anxieties about the future of our planet—of what the narrator, Jack, calls "a world spinning darker." But the bleakness of the post-apocalyptic setting is offset by instances of compassion, humaneness, and the reinstatement of small pockets of community. Skillfully wrought and shot through with a tender, lingering lyricism, Evans's novel is the work of a writer fully and satisfyingly in control of her material.

—David Medalie, Director of the Unit for Creative Writing, University of Pretoria

Elle Evans masterfully sends Jack and his dog Bud on a harrowing journey across a rural dystopia toward an uncertain technological salvation. This story melds the seemingly inevitable destruction of an American countryside with the possibility and danger of a new world ... and the brutal struggle to reach it. *Ship in the Sky* is a raw and resonant expedition into the places civilization quickly forgets—a standout work that builds in suspense and violence, delivering us from the point of destruction through the chaos of a fallen backcountry to the fragile hope for escape. In Evans's sure hand, moments of great humanity are herein combined with desperate violence in a sensitively imagined world uncomfortably close to our own.

—RON IRWIN, author of *Flat Water Tuesday*

Jack's journey across a flooded landscape shimmers in the mind long after the closing scene. In this visual and emotive text, Jack shines—his resilience, quirky humor, courage and candor. I couldn't put it down, and I can't wait for the movie.

—JOANNE HITCHENS, editor, publisher, and author of *Death and the After Parties*

SHIP
IN THE
SKY

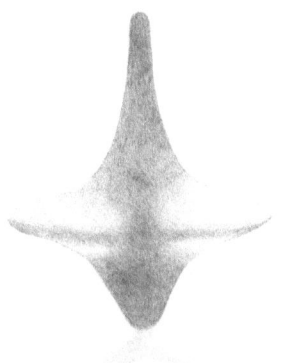

ELLE EVANS

FLARE KIDS

El Paso, Texas

Published by Flare Books, an imprint of Catalyst Press.
www.catalystpress.org

In North America, this book is distributed by Consortium Book Sales & Distribution, a division of Ingram. Phone: 612/746-2600
cbsdinfo@ingramcontent.com
www.cbsd.com

In South Africa, Namibia, and Botswana, this book is distributed by Protea Distribution. For information, email
orders@proteadistribution.co.za.

First edition, first printing
9 8 7 6 5 4 3 2 1

ISBN 978-1-963511-23-9
Library of Congress Control Number 2025936324
Spinning top illustration by Evan Marais

For you

Some say a journey starts when you leave your front door. Some say it starts far away from home, when you neither smell its scent, nor see it in your dreams no more.

Chapter One

Present Time

Am I at the beginning, ending, or somewhere in between? The way the sky looks now, I've never seen such hues. Peacock blue fanning over a line of dark chalk. Is this hell on Earth? Or Earth on hell? Or is Earth long gone and I'm standing on something else?

I'm still here and I'm walking and shifting. Or maybe things around me are shifting. It's summer-muggy, but I'm shivering something nasty. Stuck in a desert of soot-colored crud, like the soil's been caramelized on top. A thick layer of burned dirt.

And I'm seeing things.

Like this path that ain't no path. Soppy bushes flanking. Sky sizzling. Clouds dripping. Earth sponging it all up. How long's it been, this walking and watching? Walking and watching and seeing and stumbling.

Gotta get to my wristpod and dial Sky Station and find out what in God's name's happening. Gotta get home, even though home's about as comforting as a swamp of snakes. But where else am I supposed to go? I breathe deep, inhaling the sodden fumes.

Keep expecting someone behind me. Keep my senses peeled, and my imagination's doing a fine job of filling in the gaps. I'm convinced every step taken is being watched. Any minute now I'll be grabbed and pulled under and pulverized to nothing. I'm treading on two feet, my left ankle pinching but stable enough. I'm wearing Bill's gear, gone past his farm and that dead woman, and I'm heading home. Least I think I am. My brain's gone dizzy from shock.

*

An hour's passed, maybe two. There ain't a path or nothing telling me which way is where and it's twisting my insides out and my mind 'round bends I never knew existed. There's always a road. Always a trail or something that takes you somewhere, from places you know and back again. Boring as hell, but comforting to think of now that all that knowing is gone.

Hard to believe only a few days ago I was helping a sheep give birth. When I left Ma and Pa's, the Joneses made space for me, and I helped a life come forth—new hope, too—but now all that space and life are wiped. Bill and Betty were in town buying supplies, leaving me alone with Socks. Never keep livestock on my family's farm, only chickens, and they deliver their eggs neat and packaged. So I felt about as useful as a cold branding iron as Socks widened, pink and pulsing, streaks of red dripping down white wool.

I knelt close enough by, but she didn't seem to be registering anything other than the task at hand.

Then, with a sound I've never heard emanating from any animal before, she dipped her bow forward, forehead touching floor, front knees praying Amen, and grounded right there. A minute or so passed. Next thing I knew, I was holding a sack of bones in my arms, little lungs squirming for oxygen. Socks started licking its face. Long thick strokes. A nose poked through the membranes, then its whole body wiggled free, legs all angular and chopstick-thin and already starting to kick.

Dead now, all of them. Socks and her kid and Bill and Betty.

I turn about face, walk a few steps, back 'round again, then come to a halt. Someone's definitely following me. Following real close. I feel it in my bones like I feel my own veins worming through 'em. I suck in my breath. Glance back. Get ready to fight.

I spin 'round and glare at the deserted space behind me. It glares back. As does the silence. Never seen it stare so loud.

A yell from deep within me from a crazed place, wordless and rising up and out and it's long and loud and scary as fuck, and I'm barely done freaking myself out when I crouch with my arms over my head expecting someone to come flying but there's nothing. Peeping through my elbows, everything goes back to a silence even deeper than before. The worst kind of loneliness. So lonely, it feels like my whole body's being hollowed out. And my throat. That one scream had so much in it, there's nothing left to screech out, so everything's hollow inside, hollow without.

I drop to the ground heavy, knees and hands squelching in the mud. May as well end it right here. Just melt into this mess and be done with it. Been here before and there wasn't even a natural disaster to deal with, if that's what this mess is. I let my knees and hands quicksand-sink. So close to letting my head drop, so close to dropping from all fours to flat when I know I can't. Would be like trying to drown yourself, which is a damn near impossible thing to do. The only way to kill a reflex like that is to find a rock bigger and braver than you and haul it over your chest. Let something else do the dirty work and stay the hell out of your own way.

Anyway, the soil's smelling anything but pretty and I almost puke over it before lifting my head to examine the situation. One world's morphed into another and I'm crouching in a race with fuck-knows who else, with no finishing line and no starting line, either. I shudder so forcefully, I've got to hold my head from spinning.

It's the strangest thing, trying to stay calm while skidding in the slush, in this world that ain't my world, once a desert, now a flood. I've always wanted to go to the sea and I laugh a crazy kind of laugh thinking I'm finally in one but with no boat nor oar, and I've survived and surviving but what am I surviving for? My existence was small enough as it was. Only wanted to get out of farming and into the ocean, and now it's more or less come to me, and besides, if I can't find food or enough clean water then I'm gonna die of starvation or thirst or disease from not being able to wipe my own butt clean. I walk on despite all that yelling and squelching and I'm heading in the direction of home, or where that direction's always been.

This ain't fear. I've felt fear before. This here feeling is pure terrified. But I'm not collapsing. I'm stumbling more or less straight ahead, more or less where this no-path is taking me, and I realize something: people don't move forward anywhere as quickly if contentment's got anything to do with it. Contentment makes you want to lie on the earth and suck on it. It's fear that makes you leap. Far and fast to something less fearful. So I'm leaping as fast as I fucking can.

Then I see it.

The door's slamming suicidal. The rest of the house is creaking and gasping something rotten. I'm upslope from my farmstead—what's left of it, anyways—perched near its porch like a goddamn homing pigeon. Guts tightening and nerves surging, I stare from the overflowing stream to the garden and I'm staring at *my* stream and *my* garden and the skeletal remains of *my* wrecked home. Well, Jesus Christ. If that's what I've been runnin' toward this whole time then I've already lost the race.

The structure's tilted to one side, with windows popped out and shingles flown clear. Another slam and I'm scrambling down the slope, keeping my eyes peeled for any movement. The kitchen's thoroughly pulped and Ma and Pa's bedroom also, squashed beyond recognition. Only the torso of the house appears stable, though the roof's caved in like someone's socked it one. Muscles tense and slippery, I trip toward the tattered fence and open the gate.

As soon as I pass, I step on bones—dog's bones or dog bones—and an almighty crack lets loose. For a second, I think you'll both run out, screaming your heads off, but of course, that don't happen.

The gate swings shut, lopsided as a stroke. I stomp over a crisscross of flattened flower beds and lifeless branches and a minefield of dirty-clean laundry. Have to kick like a madman to release one of Pa's ties that's strangling my right foot. Overhead, the sky is streaking white and russet clouds, reminding me of pork cracklings. The rain's dripping sporadically, its taps almost turned off. I take the porch steps two by two and punch the front door open. It slaps back with a loud thud.

The quiet that follows is empty, dark, heavy. Dust swims around my eyes and I have to adjust for what seems like minutes to the stuffy hallway.

When I enter the living room, the familiar stench of cheap potpourri smacks me full-frontal. My nostrils clench in protest, and there you are, Ma, in your favorite apron, crumpled by the back door. Trying to find a way out. I walk a few steps toward you but halt, cringing at what I might see.

I turn 'round and there's your husband in his favorite position, sitting by the fireplace, face in newspaper and near enough melted into the hearth, his fists white-knuckle clenched, ready to swing. Even now, I back away from 'em.

Things are what I imagined they would be. What they always were. Yet seeing it frozen in time like this makes my heart ache.

A seething, sad anger hits me. A tidal of tears comes rising but stops at my throat. I wipe my eyes anyhow and step toward the kitchen.

I hear something. A dim groan or a low grumble and I think it's the air coagulating in the chimney or the back door swollen and moaning in the wind until a thin, scraggy ghost of a dog shuffles out of the bathroom, tail wagging. Bud's mouth is all wet and smiley. I'm guessing he's had a good drink from those leaking pipes.

Still.

How the hell did you survive all this? I ask.

He howls at me like I'm the first and last thing breathing he'll ever see. He's probably right. Part of me wants to give him a big, old hug.

And part of me wants to eat ya, I tell him as a joke, though I ain't sure he's buying it.

I squat next to him and he licks my hands. A tasty cocktail of salt, iron, and dug-up potatoes. I ruffle his fur.

We pad into the waste of the kitchen. The cupboards are bare or caved in or both. You never believed in hoarding things, Ma. Mostly picked stuff fresh from your vegetable patch. A bag of potato chips is littering the ground, so I make a grab for it, as well as for two jars of beans and one jar of peaches and a stale bread roll burrowing in the nearest cupboard. Throwing the roll to Bud, I head into the passage, past the bludgeoned bathroom, and arrive at my bedroom, its walls limp but holding steady.

The door cracks open to a crime scene. Desk lamp broken to bits, its bulb dislodged and leaking rust on the carpet. Wardrobe sprung open, clothes lying sprawled on the floorboards like bodies outlined in chalk. I rush to the bedside table. My wristpod's smashed between the wall and the bed thrown vertical against it like a stick-'em-up. I tilt the bed frame, grab the wristpod and try dialing up to Sky Station anyway. Nothing but static. Cursing, I run my fingers down the wood joints and under the mattress, finding Ma's handgun and Pa's old Navy photograph lodged in the planks. I set the photo on the bedside table, check the gun's safety catch, then place it beside the photo.

I catch my reflection in the mirror and my jaw drops. Dark lines of filth everywhere. Dried blood on my forearms and etched across my cheeks like war paint. Walnut hair tangled with darker wood and the green in my eyes a color I've never seen before—cut jade mixed with lead.

I'm not turning eighteen. I'm turning into something else.

I turn away, grab my backpack from the wardrobe, and fill it with whatever I can fit: the jars and bag of chips, underwear, shirt, socks, the gun, Pa's picture. I take Bill's clothes off and find my own raingear hanging on the hook on the door. Shove Bill's goods into my pockets. Tugging on dry socks and my own boots and galoshes, I pull my yellows over my jeans and shirt, then heave the backpack onto my shoulders. I gather the wool blanket lying in a bundle on the floor and bunch it in my arms. One last scan around my room and then I'm done.

Steering past the living room with its chaos of furniture, I get to the back door. To you, Ma. Your face is turning away from me, your eyes open. I get on my knees and wring the blanket tight. When I'm done wringing, I flare the wool over the whole of you gentle as I can.

Words come and go, so I leave them gone. In their place, grief mixed with something else. Something like relief. A last glance at Pa and I stand up and open the back door, Bud trailing. We weave through the disaster of the garden. Exit the dying gate. Before we pass the fence, I stare at my dog and he stares at me.

You know something, Buddy? I say, my words like a scratch. Anyone would think Armageddon's just happened, and I guess it would seem that way if you're looking from outside in. But from where I'm standing?

Home looks just the same.

Chapter Two

Nine hours earlier

Sky's grumbling.

Betty is busy calling across two sets of doors, say-ing food's ready. Pork with potatoes. My nostrils soak it in. I peel my eyes from the porthole-sized bathroom window and join Bill waiting at the head of the table, a pot of stew steaming on the red-and-white-patched tablecloth. Betty's tubby church candle centerpiece stands proud beside the pot, surrounded by a moat of moss with willow buds tucked in like sleeping rabbits.

Bill says grace and prays for rain. The earth's been parched all summer, he says. Nothing but stiff-ironed blue sky. Rain's needed in this valley like breath, and it looks like we might just get it now. We watch the windows turning darker, clouds crinkling and getting real moody and stirring pearly washes of paint. My fingers clench around my knife and fork when a crack of thunder ripples close.

When the rain begins to trickle, Bill suggests I take a longer break before getting back to work. The old boss is always doing kind things like that. He pours me a double whiskey for the weather turning wet and me turning eighteen. The gold burns warm and velvet along my tongue. I ain't used to spirits, so I'm tipsy in a minute. After chugging a glass of water, the room starts behaving itself, but then Betty heads back to the kitchen and Bill pours me another double measure with a finger to his lips and it's too impolite to stop, so I down the shot, feeling cozier than when Tommy and I stole that church wine when we were twelve.

Anyways, the shots are what get me walking through the drizzle to my rock. It links farmstead to forest and is always asking for a snooze, so I tuck myself in like Betty's rabbits and wait for the storm to hit.

*

Layers of gray swirl above me like teeth grinding, angry and wanting, all nap long. Two boom-clap-bangs and my drunken eyes snap open to clouds thick as clay, metal-sheet lightning, and thunder thumping close and heavy as fists. My fingers grip at the rock and I'm watching and listening, listening and watching and I'm hearing yelling and it's my own heart yelling, and I realize this ain't dreaming.

This ain't dreaming.

I ease myself near the rock's edge, hanging there like a loose tooth when the ground rips apart—clear splits thirty feet in front of me right through the Joneses' veggie patch. My gut leaps to my chest. Would be an awesome sight if it weren't so terrifying. Air, water, fire, and earth dancing into one, blasting the ground inches from the Joneses' farmhouse, splitting their flagpole, my eardrums just about exploding in the roar: thunder echoing trees cracking, water surging. Next thing, my legs are falling from my body or my body's falling from the rock and we're sinking together, sliding down. Then silence.

Earth-shattering silence.

Nothing moves, not even my lungs. I glance past my feet into a pit of nothing. Then I'm scrambling, grabbing a stone ledge above me and hauling myself over it, boots slipping, panting and cursing and wondering how a quake this size could hit my village.

Dust is hovering, brewing a soup thick and dark in the air. I raise my arms and squint at the land turned inside out. Brown clumps everywhere. Green skin peeled right off the earth, leaving raw tissue. I crank my head toward the farmhouse and it's sinking.

Come on, Bill. Get out of the house. Get the Missus and get the fuck out.

Triple-decker boom and the sky breaks open, rain belting down.

Come on, Bill. Come on, Betty.

Something collapses under my hand.

My head follows, skull on stone.

*

Whizzing in my ears. Bees. Hundreds. Whizzing high, 'round, low. I swat them away till I realize there ain't nothing but my ears doing that buzzing. And black spots in both eyes. Spots clearing to something blacker. I feel for my body, hands reaching all over for life, pulse. Aside from an ugly bump sprouting on the back on my head, plus bruises the size of beetles scattering my arms and legs, I'm intact, gasping out stale whiskey breath. I'm amazed the rock held on so steady.

How long's it been? Feels like the biggest knockout I've ever had, but a knockout just the same, so I breathe through the waking up bit, waiting for my eyes to clear before crawling across the slanting cleft, peering over the ledge to a drop two feet lower than where the ground was before. A mound of sinking sludge awaits. Clouds are hanging heavy, flooding the ground with rain like the ocean's flipped itself over.

Swinging my legs, I drop and slide a further foot before grabbing a mess of branches to heave myself up. There's some smaller rocks poking out from the mud and I stumble over them, stopping short when I see the damage beyond the tangled edge of the forest. I gawk at the farmhouse, at the gaps of land I'll have to leap over to get anywhere near that crater cradling the Joneses' stack of sticks like some big bad wolf's come and blown the whole thing down.

No sign of Bill or Betty.

Arms stretched for balance, I tread over clumps of filth and God-knows-what, calling out to them, but no sounds escape my mouth. I try again, screams breaking through now, and the whole world must be listening but no one answers, not even the livestock. No one except the hissing hail beating my beaten-up, hungover head. Can't see a single living thing.

Gotta do something fast. Gotta save Bill and Betty if there's any saving left to do. I stare at the house for a good moment or two, maybe more, gathering my thoughts, making my breathing right again. Another tick of time and any hope of finding them alive turns to something less cheerful. Looks to be only a few places I can poke through. The kitchen maybe, though it's more or less crushed beyond the doorframe. Or the hallway dumped on top of the kitchen, its orange doors an open-beaked chick squawking at the heavens.

The hallway, then.

I rise up, ringing rainwater from my clothes, then stumble toward the shingled roof which has slid down the west wall. I squat under the temporary shelter and peer through the kitchen window. All I'm seeing is dimness and dust swirling from fallen wood slats. Ducking and diving, I trip through the front door, banging my shoulders on a crippled hat stand. The hallway's groaning. A naked lightbulb's dangling on a rope from a fault line in the ceiling, swaying slight. I cringe at the sight.

I whip my head left and right, listening, though I know I'm listening for nothing. The Joneses are gone, buried somewhere under this rubble. Best case scenario they got out, made it somewhere safe. But they ain't here either way.

Side-stepping a vertical bench, the floorboards creaking under my feet, I spot Bill's yellow raingear hanging on hooks: hat, jacket, coveralls. One galosh is lodged under the bench, the other's a bathing duck near the back of the hallway, floating in a puddle where the wall's caving in on itself.

Everything's two sizes too big but I ain't complaining. I grab the galoshes and pull them over my sodden boots, then slide the coveralls and jacket over my jeans and shirt. Just in time, too, because a burp somewhere in the bowels of the house turns into a belch and the entire structure drops another foot. Last thing I see before I jackrabbit out of there is the lightbulb bomb-dropping on my shadow that's flinging after me like a goddamn demon. I skid over uneven ground and leap clear of the surrounding moat as the sky delivers up a round of hail.

Then I'm on the ground, rocking back and forth like a child and burying my nose in the collar of Bill's raincoat. It smells like pipe and shaving cream and another day's rain.

*

The wind picks up where the shakes left off, scraps of metal and roof shingles whirling. Survival instincts start kicking in. This is farm country, so mud will be everywhere. Two options: church, or Ma and Pa. My triangulation points. Strangulation points, more like. Still, they're the only ones making any sense. Town's miles away. Church only two. Ma and Pa, because it's only right.

I stop rocking and sniff the air. Never smelled

anything like it. Sweat mixed with iron mixed with kelp, and there ain't no sea for miles. I gaze upwards. No sun, no stars, no Sky Station. Nothing to navigate by. The hail's now a manageable rain and the earth seems to be settling into the mess it's made, a flood like I've never seen before. And this wind. Maybe I can find better shelter before evening falls. Hard to tell how long it's been since mayhem hit, what with my blackout too, but it's getting darker by the minute. Unsettling as shit not knowing the time of day. My wristpod's lying on my bedside table at home, minding its own time.

Hey.

Someone swaying in the vegetable patch.

Hey! I shout again.

A man with his hand torn from his wrist. Lumber-jack shirt and black trousers ragged. Strings of straw escaping his midriff. Mr. Scarecrow, staring at me, unblinking. I look past him to something being scooped up by a gale and aiming for his head. A knobby branch whipping right past. Whipping straight at mine. I duck just in time.

I'm shivering right through. My insides are swirling like this catastrophe, quakes and hail and wind. The elements are still deciding who's in charge, and I'm not keen on going anywhere till they make up their minds.

Bill's tractor's worse for wear, but standing. Stum-bling toward the dented vehicle, collecting two potatoes poking like pimples along the way, I huddle up and onto the driver's seat. I decide right there and then not to be afraid, though my insides are churning with the stuff.

I inhale deep, taking stock. Bill's Swiss Army is hiding under the seat, along with a box of matches and his stash of tobacco. I place them in the pockets of his coveralls, then consider the dirty potatoes sitting in my lap. I'm not hungry but starving and then it hits me. The storm must have knocked me out hours ago. Maybe even yesterday. I'm never this empty after one of Betty's stews. Panic whacks me then, too, right through. I try rubbing my goosebumps smooth, my body aching in places I didn't know it could and my forehead pounding like I've just been through a tumble wash. Guess I have. Closing my eyelids to the rising dread, I tell myself to get a grip, and get moving.

I swing my legs over the tractor door, knocking the potatoes. They roll like heads landing splat deep in the mud pit below. Cursing, I leave them put. Stepping down, I reel backwards, grimy water tidal-waving the galoshes. One step taken and I'm already on the back foot.

Three miles.

Three miles I gotta tread to get back home.

Releasing my squelching galoshes from the puddle, I take a moment to reorient my nerves. The Joneses' property is where the demolition site began and ended. No doubt folks in the village are enjoying their morning's breakfast, or lunch, or dinner—wherever the day is now. I'm fretting over nothing. My head's got to think this way or else I'll fret over everything.

Wrapping my arms 'round my crown, I trek through the flimsy soil, past the scarecrow, to the lane running parallel to the Joneses' property. Arriving at the toothpick remains of their picket fence, the lane turning right toward home has completely vanished. Nothing to look at but masses of upturned land, blanketed with water. Nothing to hear except rounds of hail and raindrops, punctuated with gaping pockets of silence.

Stunned, I turn left instead, head to the tractor trail just visible yonder. It leads to the village stables and acres of farmland after that. Looks like I'll be taking the scenic route home.

A hundred yards in and the trail is turning into a gutter. No sign of tracks, plus the haystacks heaped alongside are melting into thick porridge. I pull my hat strings tighter and trudge up and over the humps of hay, avoiding potholes, panic bubbling. Any step could be an inch deep, or hundreds.

I keep checking the fields for signs of civilization, for where the upchucked earth turns decent again. No such luck. The waterworks are painting everything ash anyway, sweeping and blurring my vision. The clouds are making me claustrophobic, I've never seen them slung so low. I stomp forwards toward the last of the oaks bordering Bill's land. Branches are hanging lame and broken. Trunks are compacted and splintering their own roots.

Muscles aching with effort, I plough through the soil. Each step harder, each foothold sliding more into the scum. Next step, and the world's taken right out from under me. My left leg drops five feet into a void. My right bends somewhere at the knee. The rest of me claws at the soupy topsoil. Gasping, I pull myself up and flop on the lumpy turf, then pound the earth with my fists till it feels like my heart's gonna explode. I barely notice the shot of pain stabbing my left ankle.

Damnit. I don't care so much about the pain except what it could mean. Already feeling the throb that's going to shoot to my head when I try standing up. Sucking my breath, I roll over in the mud—feeling too much like a hog—and pull my leg up with both hands, easing the galosh, boot, and soggy sock off. I know enough about broken bones to know what to look for and with relief I want to hoot at, it's only a sprain, if that. I keep my foot raised anyhow. I whisper to my ankle since I got no one else to whisper to.

I don't trust the ground no more so we're gonna crawl to that there oak and we're gonna stay put for a bit. See what passes our way. Hopefully someone helpful.

And crawl I do. Sock, boot, and galosh back on, I reach the dented and demented tree that needs a hug just about as much as me. It creaks under my clutching, or maybe that's the other oaks leaning in for support. A canopy of leaves is keeping the waterworks at bay. Not exactly a silver lining, though a lining just the same.

My thirst's grinding for attention. Resting my foot in a spoon of a root, I cup my hands and take sloppy sips from a small puddle. At least there's water. The past couple of months folks had been talking about turning the taps off and living off the wells, praying for rain day and night and all times in between. Must have prayed so hard, God turned his taps on full. I take a lungful of air. The swampy odor's hitting hard. A wet, sewer rat kind of stench.

I glance at the sky again. No way still to tell the time. No Sky Station lights blinking through. Any time and anything could be hovering above those clouds. Worry creeps in, settling somewhere in my gut. Ma and Pa. My dog. I've gotta get home.

I've gotta know.

Double boom. Thunder and lightning clapping together, a one-two sucker punch, no seconds in between. An oak to my left cracks clean down the middle. I lurch to the side as a slice of trunk splits off and thuds to the ground two feet shy of my own. My heart hops. The ground shudders. I hoist myself up and stagger from the oaks as another streak of thunder-lightning flares the sky white.

A jagged movement grabs my attention. In the near distance, a mass of heads or a monster with many is rising up and over the land and drifting closer, then tiding away. I rub my eyes. Teenagers. A tribe of, heads bobbing and bodies tiding in a surging river of mud. I make to go after them, sliding all about while they keep flowing through a field that ain't a field, finding no purchase but each other's arms and faith and the rain's too deafening for them to hear me anyway.

So I watch them go. I watch them go till they're gone, and in their place, another face.

Bill's.

He's waving at me, frantic. Shirt ripped to shreds, pants torn, he's tilting toward me, struggling over the land. Calls my name but it blurs in the gale twirling. He points to the farmstead, shouting for Betty. I reach for him, sinking in the porridge. We're fifty feet from each other. A grimace shaped like a smile and he's reaching for me, too. The rest of him frowning.

He's in bad shape. Looks like a mud monster himself. Can't believe he's still standing. And then he's not. I hobble toward him, but the mudslide's quicker.

Arms waving wild, the whole of him drops under the brownest of water and there's nothing I can do but scream and watch in horror as he merges with the rapid that's now snake-tonguing in two directions, one tongue swirling him away from sight, the other careening toward me.

Fuck. Fuck. Fuck.

I stumble back to the oaks, for a mad moment wondering what's worse, drowning or frying. A glimpse back and the river's changing tack, joining the ditch by the flattened fence meant to house horses long gone.

I catch my breath. Wipe tears from my chin. Christ, Bill. Not you.

Sweeping my eyes over the immediate surrounds, I spot the Joneses' rusty postbox dented to all hell, the little red flag pointing up in surrender. One look back to where Bill was last standing and I retrace my steps, dodging the river, forcing my way to the postbox, my stomach flipping with every thunder crack. Almost at the property when the storm decides to retreat. Wind's still howling, but the hail is light-switching off and the clouds hang, deflated. Storms catch in this valley like flies in a bowl, humming for days. Never seen nothing as ugly as this, though. Not by a long shot.

I arrive at the yard within greeting distance of the disemboweled scarecrow, now slain on the ground. Legs and arms shot from their pockets. I stumble past, avoiding eye contact, calling out for Betty in the direction of where Bill was pointing, close to the crack in the vegetable patch. I survey the wreck. She could be lying ten feet away and I wouldn't notice. The vegetable garden looks like a tossed salad minus the salad. There's bumps of land and bulges everywhere. The crack is a blackened grave.

Tying the hat strings under my chin and stitching my elbows to my ears, I zigzag closer and peer at the blackness, bile rising to my teeth. Nothing visible but roots and worms. Looking up, I clock a few corn stalks near the forest edge, wagging in the gale, naked as pigs. I make my way, ankle moaning, and trip over a decent-sized potato. I pocket it and the corn, then work my way around the back of the farmhouse. The whole left side looks worse than anywhere else. It's completely crushed. Shoulders slumped, I whisper a sorry to the Missus, then recalibrate.

Home, I think. I gotta get home.

Circling past my rock and skirting the forest is the only option left. Behind me, the river's turned into a tidal pool, swirling back in on itself. A long moment hoping Bill will bob up, smiling like he usually does. But recalibration only goes so far. I tread past the rock, tears welling again, the earth rising a little higher and dryer as I push past ground zero.

A quarter mile or so, and I do a double-take. Someone's leaning against a truck. Twenty yards yonder. A woman. Gangly and bent over, hands on her knees and eyes fixed on the ground like she's searching for something. A mop of red hair dangling over her shoulders, the ends almost touching her knees. She rises slowly and looks straight at me but then right past. I turn my head to where she's staring and there's nothing except soggy bushes and a horse plough tipped on its side. When I turn back, I'm all she's staring at. She leans away from the truck, almost falling face first in the muck. Arms reaching to her sides for balance, she staggers forth, dress hanging loose around her body, arms now locked straight in front, zombie-style. And that ain't red hair no more, but blonde streaked with blood. I step back on instinct.

Help me, she rasps, eyes glazed and staggering closer.

I stay put, ready to bolt. When she gets within striking distance, her eyes turn human and she trips forward. I just manage to reach out and break her fall. Blood smudges my forearms. There are lines of red dripping down her own. I follow the lines to a shard of glass twisted in her left ear.

Help me, she moans again.

More shards stuck in her crown as fresh dye spills. I steady her upright and she pulls her fingers through her curls like she's trying to pluck the shards out. I brush her fingers away.

Just hold on now, I tell her. Hold on.

I start digging in my pocket for something to use as a bandage when the woman sways forward, throwing me off-balance. Her matted hair parts way to a rivulet of red sliding down the right side of her neck where another wedge of glass is twisted, though this one bigger and leaving enough space for liquid to gush. An odd gurgling leaks from her throat. She landslides from my grip, sinking in an earth all too willing to swallow her up. I search the fields, frantic. There's gotta be others close by seeing this. Must be running over now to help. Why's there no one running over?

The woman's twitching now, dress soaked in crimson, face caked in dirt. She's looking sideways, away from me, and I want to look away too, but I can't, 'cuz I'm all she's got.

It's okay, I whisper, kneeling and placing my hands on her shaking shoulders. It's okay.

A gasp for breath, one last twitch, then stillness. Except for the blood. The woman's blood's alive, blooming color into a world gone dead and still busy dying.

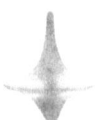

Chapter Three

Present Time

Fucking potholes.

I keep checking my pockets, feeling through the waterproof fabric for the stuff that's gonna keep me and Bud alive out here. No idea how far the destruction's spread out, and it's getting harder to make like everything's just fine when everything I come across ain't. I've tripped up so many times, I wouldn't be surprised if half my belongings were sprinkled behind us, hidden in the sludge like Hansel and Gretel crumbs. Though I ain't planning on following them home. Home no longer exists.

It strikes me then, the thought that I've got nothing to go back to. Nothing to protect. Nothing home-wise to fear. All the sudden the ground I'm treading on seems less treacherous, the sky less ominous, even with Sky Station not yet visible. Must be up there still, must still be informing whomever to do whatever to help.

I pat Bud and he perks up, and next minute we're practically Dorothy and Toto, skipping along our yellow mud-brick road. Haystacks are leaning at friendly angles, I head toward them for cover, Bud hobbling close. Do a stock take and everything's accounted for. My attention turns to my stomach.

Only takes a couple days for hunger to burn, don't it?

My dog lifts his head. Wags a touch. I give him a rub and unzip my backpack, pull out the packet of chips. Tearing the top with my teeth, a few topple and Bud nosedives. I throw him a couple more, then tilt the bag and chew mouthfuls, the BBQ flavor salting my tongue.

I've already decided what me and Bud are gonna do: find the coast. What I was planning on doing after my stint at Bill and Betty's, once I'd earned enough money. And this flood may link us right to it. All I gotta do is find a boat. And if I can't find a boat, if this disaster's gone further than local and slid the coast-line into everything else, well, I'll just dive into the makeshift sea and float away till I sink under. Figure by that stage I won't even need a rock. Giving up will be easy.

I zip up my backpack. Rain's dripping like it can't help itself, like a child still learning to potty-train. Who knows when it'll stop for good.

Night's coming, I tell Bud. Gotta find us a shed or something.

Leading us on, something rises in my gut—the same creepy-crawly feeling I had when I was walking toward home. I do a one-eighty and scan the fields. Nobody. Just a truck half-sunk in the muck, one of the doors ajar.

Shaking my head, I continue. A hundred yards on, I stop again.

Come out. I know you're there.

Silence.

Come on, now. I'm waiting.

I try keeping the tremor out of my voice. The feeling's Halloween-spooky and I know I'm not making it up, because Bud's ears are pricked. He's looking toward the forest, the edge of which I've been using as a marker.

I reach into my pocket for my gun, turn left, and start treading where Bud's pricking. I've got a weapon and I'll sure enough use it, had enough target practice using Pa's beer cans. We're almost at the edge of pines when a rush of sound erupts—twigs snap, leaves rustle and whoosh, out springs something animal and attacking.

I spin 'round. Run as quick as I can, toward the truck, diving into the driver's door swung open like a gift. Bud leaps too. I thrust him onto the passenger seat. Slam the door shut. The beast's charging so fierce, it bangs into the hood. The car jolts and shudders. Something silver flashes. The beast goes down.

I clench my gun and open the door slow. Inhale sharp. It *is* a beast, lying on its side, tongue lolling, pupils glossy, teeth white protruding. The bash into the hood must have felled it. Not for long, I'm sure. But there's also a knife—stuck in the ground two feet from its shoulder. Silver blade, bone handle.

I blink from the blade to the bison, not believing it's

a bison, but it must be. Never seen one up close. Never seen one anywhere. I sit shock-still for what seems an age, nerves flying all over the place, waiting for the guy behind the knife to show, deciding what to do about the hunchback. Since the world's gone so topsy-turvy, for all I know, the animal could have been either attacking or fleeing. And now that I think about it, was the blade aimed at him, or me?

Fuck this.

Stay put, I warn Bud, and step out of the car, kicking the mound of soggy grass from the bottom of the door frame till it gives completely. I keep it ajar and crouch down, one eye pinned on the forest, the other on the bison. This one's huge. Maybe they all are. Bulbous head. Humped back. A carpet of fur laid over his upper body, a fine layer over his lower. Pug nose and small eyes and thick horns curving. It's panting heavy, eyes panicked.

I try thinking straight, mustering courage, but nothing much musters. Could do with owning a knife bigger than Bill's fingernail file. Could do with the other guy not. I tip-toe 'round, then closer, the bison watching every step. His gums wet and dripping spit. Tail twitching. Least I've got the gun. I make a show of it, holding it steady as I can with my trembling hands, swinging it 'round, sure now someone's watching.

A ton of licks when I return to the vehicle. I smear Bud's gob on the black leather seat, feeling equal parts wise and foolish. Leaning back on the headrest, the Ford's in great nick, considering. Luxury model.

All dolled up with nowhere to go. I stare at the key stuck in the ignition. It's got a good-luck rabbit's foot dangling from the keyring.

What the hell do we do now? I mutter.

Looking out and over Bud's head toward the passenger window, I survey the shitstorm strewn 'round. The visuals: upside-down fields, sky as gray as old soup, rivers overflowing like cuts with too much pus. The audibles: Bud's antsy panting and some nearby birds chittering bright and cheerful. Robins, by the sounds. I imagine their chests puffed out and rosy, cheering us on or mocking us silly.

I spot something in the rearview mirror. A blade of sorts in the far distance, its silver-tipped end pointing up. A church spire. *My* church spire. Never been so glad to see it. If we can make it over without being speared or trampled, then we'll have more than enough shelter for the night.

Bud, we're going that-a-way, I say.

Glancing at the lame bison and silent forest beyond, I ease the passenger door open and scoop Bud in my arms. The wind's helping mute our movements. I carry him over the frame and onto the soggy ground like a thief carrying a treasure chest.

Bud tries squirming out of my grip.

Shhh, I whisper. I know what I'm doing.

Which is a more or less a lie as I've never been doing what I'm doing now. But I keep doing it, sidestepping, keeping the car between us and the forest. I'm watching the woods and the church and the dog and the truck and my feet. I give up on the sidestepping, release Bud, and we and make a break for it, running wild toward God's house. After a minute, we're far enough away to risk a look back. The Ford's a rusty boulder in the near distance, the bison a heaving stone. Same scene, only in miniature, but one thing's missing. The knife.

Chapter Four

We tread on. Fast.

I release Bud and boot it toward Hawk Hill. Ascending will give us an advantage, plus the ground's turning bog with every step so the best way across is up. We're through the first layer of muck when my feet trip over something bulbous and brown camouflaged in the soil, a pack of flies hissing in protest. Tentative, I poke my boot into a body clogged with fur. Badger, or hare. I exhale, relieved it ain't human. Bud comes to inspect but I tell him to back off 'cuz the stench shouts poison. One step to my left and I almost trip again over another bulbous something. I hop clear of the gravesite.

As I do, Bud charges ahead, splatting soil on my yellows. We trek up the hill, no sight or sound of anyone following. Hawk's a small enough hike to manage in one go, so we haul it to the top where I do a three-sixty. I'm looking at chaos. A crater filled with wildly rushing rainwater is stretching from the churchyard all the way to the forest's edge. Looks like a meteorite has crashed clear across it. Cars are apple-bobbing in the water. A horse trailer is tipped over the closest edge, its winged doors hanging open. Further along, on the other side of the cavity, a horse is leaning askew, comatose.

My heart pounds in disbelief. Earthquakes never happen in Overstraddle.

I walk the short way over to the westside and the village below is unrecognizable. Tim's hardware shop is almost flattened. The library's flooded. I blink twice at three middle-aged folks walking in a tight knot along the main road, dodging a swamp. The woman's holding what looks to be a cat. The two men are carrying knapsacks.

Hey! I yell.

One of the men slows his pace, releases from the knot. Spots me waving. An ounce of time and he shakes his head, shuffling back to the others. I'm a blip in their slow parade. Out of everything, that's about the scariest thing I've witnessed so far. People too bewildered to stop.

I yell louder, alarm etching my throat.

Any news on what's happening?

The other man, big and burly, turns around.

Nothing, he shouts up. Remaining folks are stationed at the Town Hall. Floods are worse that side, though. People are panicking.

Ship ... Sky Station? I shout back.

The man scratches his beard.

Glitching. Communication's sure down.

I shift on my feet.

Got family due south, he continues. With a farmstead holding steady. Would say to join us, but you seem the panicking type to me. Town Hall's waiting, if you are.

His glare's puncturing, just like my old man whenever he got going. I hold my ground.

So? he says.

So what? I answer.

You gonna join us, or go that-a-way?

I tighten my lips, pat Bud's head. My dog gazes at me with his wide, chocolate eyes.

Come on, I say, quiet. Let's go.

I shake my head slow, turn 'round, motion me and Bud down the other side of the hill. We descend together, the church looming into view. This close, the spire's an upside-down sugar cone set into mounds of melted ice cream. The entrance and the Sunday school section are smashed. The main body's still standing, though sunken.

Wonder what God would make of that heap? I ponder aloud.

My raingear's near enough plastered to my skin. I pour out my galoshes, turning my focus to the massive ditch of water writhing dark and angry between us and that spire, plotting a way around it.

Bud's beside me, nipping some mud clots from his paws. His ribs stick out from his wet fur.

They even feed you while I was away? I ask.

He ignores me and starts trotting.

When we get about a stone's throw from the chapel's

entrance, I realize we got no choice other than to go through the water. No point walking around to the back of the church. River Wren, the largest in the county, runs there and is probably overflowing into this fresh one, the mouth of which is yawning into the drenched rose garden, right up to the wrought iron gates. From this distance, I think about calling out for survivors but any sound will only blend with the surge of rainwater.

I spot the narrowest bit of the ditch about ten feet closer to the gates and lead us toward it. I take off my rain jacket and pull my backpack straps tight 'round my shoulders, zipping my jacket over the whole of it. I take off my socks and pocket them, pulling my boots, then galoshes back on over my bare feet. I roll up my jeans.

I tell Bud what we're about to do. He sniffs the edge of the rushing river and backs up a bit when he sees me dip a toe. After a few feet, there ain't nothing to see but oily blackness.

It's okay, Buddy. We go steady. Twenty or so feet is all we gotta do.

I take a hesitant step into the shallows. I figure my dog won't do the leading, and if I look back, he won't follow. I'm halfway across, the water level no higher than my shins, before Bud finishes his whining and pads in. I turn 'round to watch. Current's rising to his neck. Fur fanned like a dirty mop.

Come on, now.

My words slide away the same moment my balance

does, feet dropping right out from under me like fishing line anchors. Down, down, down into blackness like I've just fallen of a cliff and near enough. There's shallow ground toward the other side, near the shoreline, but too late. This gap has me, pulling me south. The shock and jerk of the undercurrent suck my galoshes right off. Two seconds later they're bobbing up to the surface—giddy ducks dipping and diving near Bud's head, and whether instinct or a game of fetch kicks in, he springs after one. Next second, he's rushing right past, the current catching us both and him spinning around me, a galosh in his canines.

I yell at him, water tipping into my lungs. Bud's eyes are scared and his legs are scrambling for a swimming angle. His head's ducking under the current and the galosh is filling and tugging him down further. Games are all gone as far as he's concerned and I've got to act quick. Sweet-and-sour slime fills my mouth again as I front-paddle, coughing and spurting, my rain jacket bulging and blocking my vision. I grab for his neck and yank the boot instead. Bud careens further down the current and I watch his ribs slam hard into a spin-bottling branch.

Grab on! I tell him, though I'm telling us both, having lost all bearings of where's deep and where's shallow and where's that dog. Losing sight of him in all the twirling and whirling and we're turning a corner in that twisty tunnel death-trap and I'm seizing a spine of a tail and a spindly crustacean body and I'm towing and hauling and suddenly we dock to a complete stop,

Bud's back on my belly and his legs flailed up like an upturned crab.

We lay there wheezing in the shallows. Then Bud squirms and coughs up something slimy over my chest. I push him off.

I sit up, gawking at the church, now within crawling distance. The river has curved us right up to its backside. And this really is God's house of miracles, 'cuz my galoshes have somehow washed up, too. I pull them on, water squelching. I reach behind me, patting my back. The pack's still there. Smushed flat, but intact.

I lift my dog in my arms and leap to shore before either of us can decide on doing anything else, telling him I've got it from here. He licks my cheek and his muscles go limp, though his eyes keeping darting left and right for signs of danger. Bud's not as lightweight as he was before, or maybe my arms ain't as strong as they usually are, but by the time I get past the ditch to the chipped-to-bits graveyard, the whole of me is exhausted. Outsides soaked and insides starved. I lower Bud to the ground, swearing some rotten.

It's not you, I tell him. It's everything.

He pays no heed and limps ahead, weaving through the maze of gravestones before halting and cocking a leg over a broken one. The wind's stronger on this side, howling at the headstones like they're gonna domino-drop any second, like all God's gotta do is give 'em a pinky-push. There's holes the size of dugout graves where the overflowing River Wren's tipping over and into them. On second look, they *are* dugout graves.

Am I imagining it, or are those coffins peeking out of the soil?

Graveyards ain't spots for visiting at the best of times and my imagination ain't a spot for visiting at the worst, so I'm not gonna hang around any longer than necessary in this creepy-as-shit boneyard. I force my eyes to the church. Can't hear nobody inside.

A crunch behind me. I spin 'round and Bud's dangling a gristly knuckle of bone like he wants to play tug-of-war. I swallow bile and look sideways in disgust.

I tread over what's left of the stone path, enter the building, do a sweep of the dank interior. Most of it's been damaged by the flood—swollen timbers and stone columns toppled. Nothing flies at me except empty silence. Silent as The Almighty himself. My heart pumps relief and disappointment all at once.

Anyone here? I ask the emptiness.

It answers in dying echoes.

Bud darts past and skids to the pews, sniffing each row and then the red carpet snaking up the aisle. Following him, I wade through a wash of water and glance up at the stained-glass windows, breathing in the greens and blues and golds.

Wrapping my arms around my chest, a haunted chill starts seeping deep. I turn in a circle, slowly, making sure nothing's gonna spring out at me. Startle when I see a man hanging from a roof beam at the other end of the church, naked except for a loincloth plus nails dug into his palms and feet. A second look to make sure he ain't real. Wonder for a second if he ever was. Wonder not for the first time how a man could ever go through such a thing as to end up pinned to a tree. His eyes are gazing at his feet and beyond them, and I almost ask him how he does that—make a divine being's suffering look so human.

Leaving him in peace, I turn back to the pews and strip off my clothes. Shed them like unwanted skin. Then I peel off my backpack, place the contents on a pew, and take stock. If this is all we've got to live on, we ain't gonna be living for long. My world has become what's existing on this bench. A closing-in of, and a rapid shrinking.

Shoulders slumping heavy, bones shivering in the clammy dampness, I sigh loud and place my bits in a line. Count and turn each item over, then place them back again, putting Bill's jackknife in my outside pocket for easy reach. Smelling the tobacco is making me shaky hungry so I pinch a wad and plop it on my tongue then tuck it into my cheek like how Bill does.

Did.

Digesting all that honey-cedar richness through my gums is a momentary satisfaction until the door we traipsed through slams shut, turning everything black.

I jump back. Eyes fixed on shadows. Fear oozing like a wound. Shins colliding with Bud's hind legs. We scatter like spiders.

Git, I bark at him, shooing him away.

Panic's deciding things for me now, rippling like that

crater-tide. I surge toward the pulpit and hide behind it, expecting knife-man to come running. When nothing happens, I search the lectern cupboard, frantic. There must be something in here to lessen the creep and lighten the place up. First drawer I open and two candles roll forwards. Hallelujah. I lift one out along with a large box of matches.

I tell myself to get a grip before anyone else does. With trembling fingers, I try lighting five or six matches before one strikes. Searching for a candle holder, I find one right under my nose, next to a wilting bouquet of flowers. I twist the wax into the holder while noxious smoke rises. The flame makes a halo of Bud's head. He's pawing a mound of gum near the second row of pews.

Nerves settling, I spot a stash of dry logs stacked for the ready in the fire grate chiseled into the north wall. I grab my clothes, then walk back to the fireplace and throw the wet bundle, plus footgear and socks, over the stone floor in front of the grate. I light the logs with the matches and start drying myself off, thinking about the timings of things, the basics of what I've got to do now versus what I would be doing on a normal day, like eating a proper meal and showering a proper shower and sleeping a proper sleep.

I'm realizing right here and now that I've lost all bearings of ordinary actions and time slots. I'm watching the flames catching and dancing and my thoughts are doing the same. They're rushing over the last couple of days, then ahead to the next few, and

I'm wondering what we're gonna find next, and more concerning, what we're not gonna find, and even more frightening, what's maybe trying to find me.

Bud pads over, tail between his legs. He raises his paw to my hand with a tongue clacking madly. I lower to my knees and hold his muzzle open, then pry the gum from the roof of his mouth. I'm about to throw it into the fireplace when I realize it's not gum but something flat and oval and egg-white. What do ya know.

I head straight back to the pulpit, a memory flashing of Priest Bell placing his box of communion wafers in the bottom cupboard. About to pull the handle when I see it's bolted with a flimsy lock. I grab my gun from the pew and return to the cupboard. Click the safety. Aim to shoot. Then think about it. A butt-naked boy pointing a gun at a pulpit. What would the neighbors think? Besides, no sense in drawing attention from anything outside, or scaring the crap out of Bud. I lower the gun onto the open Bible splayed on top of the lectern.

Next, I bang the lock with my fist. It snaps off, rust flaking to the floor. A second later and I'm practically leaping for joy. There's a plastic tub half full of wafers, and behind it, an uncorked bottle of wine. I pull it out and jam the head of my gun on the cork. It plops and splats into the ruby juice. The first swigs swim straight from my hollow stomach to my brimming brain. I saunter down the steps with the wafers in one hand, the bottle in the other, and sit on the pew with Bud at my feet.

No wine for you, my friend, but these we can share. Hell, it's your first communion.

I lower a wafer to his muzzle. He swallows it as though I've given him nothing at all.

Yep. Wafers are about the thinnest, no-nothing wisps of air you can ever imagine eating, but I'd be grateful, Buddy. This is consecrated stuff.

I place a few on my tongue and chase them with some swigs while Bud raises his paw for more, drooling and leaning real close. I wipe the spit from my knees and look him in the eye.

Okay, this is how it's gonna go. Three for me. One for you. My belly's bigger, plus I saved your skinny ass from that river, so you owe me.

I give him a wafer and plop three onto my tongue. Must admit, they're tasting more than palatable with this wine. Before I know it, the tub's near to empty and most of the bottle's gone. I sashay to a wooden bench near the west wall—feeling well and truly consecrated and about to drop into a welcome doze—when I hear slurping. Bud's drinking from the baptism bowl on the other side of the pulpit. Peeling myself from the bench, I hobble over and cup my hands, but not before crossing my forehead and temples, just for show.

Out the corner of my eye, I spot the confession booth and walk over curious, while Bud skitters past and curls his drenched self into a donut by the fire.

Never been in the confession booth before and I ain't sure if I'm sitting in the priest's chair or the sinner's 'cuz both sides look the same to me. But I start speaking anyhow, my fingers wrapped around the bottle. I down the last swigs, then hold it up as evidence. Start confessing.

Excuse me, Father, for I have sinned. Drunken this entire bottle of wine here and haven't saved any for the rest of my life. But seeing as that could mean a couple of days, week tops, I figure you'd be in an understandin' mood. And, by the way, while we're on the subject of dying and destruction, some indication of what the fuck's happened would be mighty handy, 'cuz I've trekked too much already, and there ain't no folks about, and I got no clue how far this shitstorm stretches. So, if you could get back to me at some point between now and now, well, that'll be just dandy.

I tap the little window and slide it open and peer at nothing but dark space. I lean my head through and rest my chin on the window frame and whisper low.

One more thing, Father. If you could place another flask of wine somewhere in this vicinity by morning, plus a few more of those paper-thins for the road, I'd be most humbly grateful.

I tip an imaginary hat toward Him and sit there for a while feeling particularly comfortable. Skin warm, insides warmer, and my left hand on something even warmer still. I start stroking, feeling real good and real sinful all at once. At least I'm in the right place to confess. Still. I stand up and poke my head around the door frame in case anyone's decided on making an appearance. 'Cuz coming across a kid stroking his way to Heaven in a confession booth might be even more scandalous than coming across a butt-naked boy holding a gun at a pulpit. And for the first time since disaster has struck, I start howling with laughter, which dampens the mood, and besides, my bladder's gone near full as that crater.

I stumble out of the booth and take a sloppy piss over the rim of the wine bottle, then head toward the fire. Grab my dried rain jacket and wrap it snug around my shoulders. Eyeing Bud's cozy curl, I stuff the rest of my raingear under my sleepy head and make like a donut, too. Wind's beating stronger against the church but I'm barely registering. Eyelids heavy with exhaustion and drink, I wrap my arm 'round Bud and watch the flames till there's nothing left to focus on except the ashes of my dreams.

*

Thump thump thump ... punches so hard I can't breathe no more. My body's ducking. My mind's rattling through exit points. I reach for the desk lamp and smash it over Pa's head. Lightbulb shards pierce my nail-beds. Blood drools down my wrist and over his bald spot like an egg's been cracked. Then I'm stumbling and running through my bedroom door.

Last thing I see is glass sprinkling Pa's eyebrows.

Last thing I hear is, I'm gonna kill your ass!

I sprint into the woods with my left hand tucked tight and hide out under a chopped tree for a long while. Then I haul ass to the shed as fast as I can. It's around midnight and the night air's fucking freezing. Inside the wooden hut, all's quiet and hush except for some owls tooting and one heart hooting. I shuffle myself into a potato sack and wrap my cut-up hand in one of Ma's handkerchiefs tugged quick from the washing line.

I'm about to nod off good and proper when the shed door nudges open. I near enough shit my pants till I recognize Bud's black-as-coal nose breaking and entering my secret hiding spot. He's found me. Probably smelled the blood, too. He treads over, sniffing the whole of me before lying near my chest. Bud's found me, so I pull him close and spoon his body.

A hot water bottle for an ice-cold night.

Chapter Five

I jolt upright, disoriented, thinking of punches and sheds and springing out of them fast. But this ain't a shed, it's a church, and I've woken from one horror show straight into another. Shots of rain are dripping over my naked body, coming through the wooden beams above. Looks like the roof might give up its fight soon. I open my jaw and stick my tongue out to catch drops.

Worry shudders in. How long has that rain been falling? How much land is still around to travel on? And how easy can we move past that door we just came through? I almost barf right there just thinking of the day ahead, but hold it in and grab my clothes from the stone floor and tug them on, shivering.

My dog's by the pulpit, slurping away, but when I walk over to inspect, it's only wet drops hitting a puddle behind a broken stone pillar.

Bud?

I search the back of the pulpit and the back of the church, check behind the stone coffins, underneath the choir pews, doors, gaps that may lead outside, but nothing. I turn 'round and head back to the pews by the door we came through. It's a hair's length ajar, morning light now peeping. Wind must have knocked it open. I call out for him again.

*

Once my dog got lost. Or maybe it was me being lost. Couldn't tell 'cuz I was nine and he was hopeless and we were circling 'round each other like mosquitos 'round a net. I kept calling and searching and losing track of that tinny whimpering. Painful in its pleading, irritating in its misleading. Turns out we were not yards from each other the whole time. Got himself trapped in a side-tipped garbage bin and could scamper free any moment, but wouldn't due to a clot of kittens skirting around the edge. From where he was crouching, they probably looked like five versions of that giant cat who almost ate him up when he was a pup.

When I finally happened upon him, shooing the kittens away from a game of dead-mouse-tossing, I gave him a smack on his muzzle. Well, a pretend smack, being so worked up with him being so worked up over nothing. I slapped the air instead, then his rump, and told him to never leave my sight when we went adventuring.

There's scarier things than felines out there, I said.

He seemed to get the gist as he's never veered more than a swimming pool's length since. But that was in another world in another time and frankly, I'm surprised we haven't lost each other already given the circumstances. I'm worried as fuck, trying not to over-react, reassured by the memory of him waiting for me at home like I told him to when I went off to Bill and Betty's. So, he better be returning from wherever he's gone and find me right here.

*

About to shout out for him again when I spot a furry shape crouching under the pew where I inspected my bits upon arrival. He's licking the floor. I stomp right up.

Don't ever not come when I call ya. Thought you knew that. And you stealing now, too?

He scuttles out, strings of tobacco hanging from his gums. I do a double take. My backpack's gone—the pew's bare except for a jar of beans. I pick the tobacco packet off the floor. Bud's hardly digested any, but what's left of the brown mound is covered in gobby slime. I toss it aside and pocket the beans, then spin 'round, rubbing my head, rewinding the tape of events: backpack and bits placed on this pew. Bottle of wine downed on the other pew.

Wine.
Wafers.
Gun.
Pulpit.
Shit.

I sprint through my migraine toward the pulpit, finding the silver metal glinting darkly on the lectern. Misty morning light sprinkling over it. I pick up the gun and matches and slot them in the inner pocket of my raingear, patting my jackknife in the other. Small consolation. I charge to the door, ducking in every nook I can find, looking for the thieving bastard who took my pack.

Fear's turning to anger back to fear. Don't know if the thief is someone new or that same someone who's been following me. I keep looking over my shoulder. Bud's following my tracks, sniffing, getting nothing. By the time I return to the door, he's on my heels and getting on my nerves. Stinks like wet carpet, besides.

I push the thick wood door open and smell fouler things. A ditch that looks half moat, half sewage tunnel is flowing by, full of soil and filth. A mini-crater in itself, I can't see how anyone got into the church, or how anyone could get out, other than swimming along with the current and joining the river at the cemetery gates where the flower garden used to be. The intruder must have entered before it got bad. We've gotta leave before it gets worse.

Can't have gone far, I tell Bud. And when that asshole comes 'round next, he won't know what's coming.

Least I sound brave.

I glance right toward the graveyard. Most of the tombstones have dislodged out of their sockets, leaving a gaping mouth of broken teeth and gummy mounds. The marked earth is now unmarked. Forgotten. Blank-slated. Beyond the graveyard, well, there's nothing much to say 'cuz there's nothing much to see except new rivers flirting with the old one. Oblivious to anything wanting to stand still.

My eyes catch on something large and cumbersome drifting by my feet. A vacant coffin, roof ripped off entirely. Tipping this way and that. Drunk on fluid. It's about to pass us by when its bow lodges in the bank of mulch. My insides churn with wine and rotting dread and I upchuck right over it, not meaning to, but having to just the same. I turn my face to the wind, raindrops smearing my cheeks clean and sliding sideways into my ears, sideways onto an earth slipping away and vanishing, caring little for the living and even less for the dead.

I wipe my cheeks and act quick before the coffin dislodges. Grabbing the stone pillar flanking the door frame, I reach my foot out and manage a toehold. Edging the casket backwards, I grab the copper handle and heave the hull up and onto the top step of the entrance, the ache in my head tossing and turning like the current. Takes an age to tip it but when I do, out spills buckets of water.

Then I tell Bud to jump in. He looks at me like I'm mad, and I might be getting there, but the only way we're getting out of here is by coffin.

Swim or float, I tell him. Your choice.

Eyeballing me for a second, he raises both paws to the rim. I lift his back legs up and over before he changes his mind.

Good boy. We gotta go down this offshoot toward the River Wren, which will take us to the coast. That's what we gotta do.

Bud looks about as convinced as I feel.

I peek my head 'round the doorframe again to make sure there ain't any last-minute alternatives, my fringe plastered to my forehead. Damn rain. At least the sun's making more of an appearance, a highlighter smearing across the Wren.

There's movement behind me. Bud's pouncing out of the boat before I even think to grab hold. He darts back into the church, wriggles under a pew, head locked on his paws, going nowhere. I watch him watching me. Stepping toward him slowly, I lower and level my gaze with his. Take some moments to consider, to make my words mean something.

Thing is, Buddy, we're in this together and you ain't giving up now. We gotta keep courage. Keep going. Remember my hiding spot on the farm? The shed? Remember Tommy?

Bud raises an eyebrow.

When I was little, before you showed up, me and Tommy used to play games. Treasure hunt, tag, hide-and-seek. We'd tear around the yard, weave through the forest, shout and holler where we were, where we weren't.

Once, when I was hiding in the shed, Tommy yelled, The sky is falling! The sky is falling!

He was sick of not finding me, so he tried scaring me instead. I shot straight out of my secret spot with the shed door banging like a monster and held my hands over my head waiting for the weight of the world to flatten me. I tumbled outta my cave into the midday sun and heat and wind and thought, This is it. I'm gonna die, right here, right now.

My eyes burned, my body bent double, I near enough fell flat on the grass I felt so claustrophobic, done. Then Tommy screamed in my ear, Gotcha! Well, I sprang up and near as good clapped his ear off with my stronger hand until he pleaded mercy. He never joked about it again.

But here's the thing. When I spit myself out of that shed, Bud, I was ten going on dead, and figured it wasn't a half-bad thing, dying—not after I had gotten over the shock of it, which took about a second. Growing up all bent and beaten on a lonely farm on an overcrowded planet, I was half-finished already, so who was I to get all worked up about the world giving up the ghost?

And now that the sky *has* fallen and everyone's either dead or scrambling around like vermin, and me and you've been stumbling in rust-ridden mud pits, over potholes and other holes, bodies and other bodies, famished, itching all over, *spent*, I'm wondering— if I was okay to die back then, why am I clinging to life now? Why are you? No offense, Buddy, but you're a near-to-nothing drowned rat risen from some God-forsaken cesspool. Jesus, I can barely look at you no more. And Jesus knows what I look like cause he's not looking at me at all.

But we *are* clinging and that's gotta mean something. Something's makin' us cling. So we can't give up now. We gotta keep on going. Navigating down that river's our only chance. We're not tempting fate, we're fighting it, and I believe it may be the first time I've ever done such a thing. Now it's your turn. You gonna fight, or you gonna flight?

Chapter Six

I rise up slowly and turn back to the coffin, make like I'm busy with the satin sheeting—padding it here and there—then step into the hull. A couple of minutes pass before I hear movement across the floorboards. Nodding in his direction, I speak soft, still fiddling.

So I'll do the steering, you do the sitting. I'm gonna lift you in, then push us off somehow, and then I'll hop in after ya. Don't even worry about all the wet. The more the better at this stage. Give us more river to play with.

I glance 'round and grab a plank of wood lying in the near corner. Bud sits on his haunches, then sidles up a bit closer when I return. I take the cue and lift him up and in.

See, you don't even smell that bad up close, I say, keeping a hand on his neck and breathing through my mouth.

I step one foot into the middle of the casket and leave one foot out, pushing with my free hand until the box plunges into the water. I arch my leg over and shove Bud between my thighs. The coffin pitches, trying to balance itself, the white satin lining shiny against the surrounding scum. Water keeps sloshing in and I keep bucketing it out. Have to crouch dead center with my dog snug tight the whole time.

In a flash of movement, we spin away, tossing and rolling, but upright. I glance back at the wooden door and it's still wide open, stuck between a stubborn willow branch and the second step. The church roof looks like a giant soaked wafer. By tonight it may give completely and the stone floor will flood, pews parted by a floating red sea carpet.

Returning to the task at hand, I hold the plank clumsily above Bud's head and let the current do most of the work till we get to the gates. Then I've got to twist and turn us past the flattened flower garden and into the wider Wren.

I've always wanted to set sail. Told Bill as much when I began working for him. He didn't need any help with the farm—was managing fine himself—but he and Betty took one look at the bruises on my jaw and opened their door. Someday, I told him, I was gonna go home, pack my things, and train it as far as I could, all the way to the sea. Find a boat. Keep on going.

And look at me now—taking the helm in a coffin. Not exactly what I had in mind.

I gaze back the way we escaped from, an uneasy feeling creeping into my upchucked belly. I ain't sure who or what, but something's still lurking. I stare at the mound of church drifting away from us. A black dot on the horizon. A lost ship sailing nowhere, its tilted mast spiking the air. Its anchor line somehow umbilical-cording my gut, tugging and pulling. I shudder at the feeling, wanting clear of the ghosts haunting that place. Of the ghosts haunting me. I squeeze my dog's ribs with my knees, turn my eyes forward.

We're doing just fine, Buddy. We've ditched that thief and we'll get to the coast eventually. Just need to find some food and a bit of help along the way.

Sighing heavy, I keep balancing and moving us forward. All sorts of junk passes us by—tires, cookery utensils, swollen books. Bud pokes his head out for a bit of sightseeing as we skirt the eastern side of the forest, past one decrepit farm after another. Hunger comes rumbling. When the river turns a slow bend, I dig into my pocket for the jar of beans. Have to act fast as the coffin's still rocking. I'm about to unscrew the lid when Bud jerks, knocking it clear out of my grip. I grab for it like a man possessed, and it ricochets off my frantic fingers into the river, our boat almost toppling in the process. The jar sinks immediately.

Damnit.

I glare at Bud, then yank him back to my thighs, then spot what he's spotting. Beavers. Building a dam of sorts on our port side. Doing what they always do. I keep one grip on my antsy dog, the other on the oar, and we watch as one beaver paddles back and forth with sticks and branches while the other keeps house. They don't so much as blink at us, but I'm so distracted by the sight of them, I almost don't see the rowboat a quarter mile downstream, docked along the shore.

My belly and muscles need a pit-stop. I jiggle Bud free of my hold and maneuver the plank toward the artery, using all my might against a stubborn current that's come to life and pulling us the other way. I think for a split second about who to chuck out first, then toss Bud, telling him to jump to shore. I leap out after him, feet finding ground. I grab at the coffin but it bottle-spins and hurtles away.

My knee scrapes something hard as I curse my way up the slope. I stand up and rub my torn skin. Bud steps close and licks the patch. I step past him toward the rowboat, expecting a hamper of sandwiches or something as civilized, but it looks long-deserted and there's nothing in its belly apart from an oar lying flat along the floorboards.

Hands on my hips, I turn toward the thinning forest. There's a clearing beyond where sunlight's trickling in. I lead us over upturned roots and under downturned branches, leaving the pines behind. There's no one around. I breathe deep. Something about the rain falling soft and the sun splintering the sky, the pine needles making everything hush like they always do, makes me relax a little. To be left alone is something I've always wanted. Not *this* left alone, but for a moment, even with my stomach screaming for company, the rest of me's settling down a bit.

Then as quick as that feeling comes, it scatters. Flies right on by. Bud snaps his head a second before I do. Something rustling in the distance. Bigger than a bird, smaller than a man, larger than my imagination.

Who's there? I call out, body spinning 'round.

Maybe a dart of something, maybe a flutter right over there behind that bloated bush. Bud kinks his paw. Freezes. Whether he's frozen in fear or still assessing, I can't tell, but I step toward the sound, glad for once that Pa shoved me into the boxing ring.

*

In our neck of the woods, you can start fighting early, which means you can hit someone dead before you hit puberty. That fight I won, I was fourteen going on starving, almost as starving as now. Can practically hear Pa shouting at the top of my head. A muffled shout. Far away and far too close. A fuzzy foghorn blasting in, blasting out.

My face was stuffed in his belly in our corner of the ring, smelling his sweat, my gloves not even able to wrap 'round his waist. I hung them on his hips till he pushed them down. Then he grabbed my upper arms and it was a welcome relief to be held up like that, almost off the floor. A dangling puppet. The position made my chin drop and my attention swim to my boxing shoes, and I always thought that was something—how boxing shoes can stay so white despite what's going on above 'em. Like butcher's gloves before a slaughter.

You gotta give him more than that, Pa spat.

He fired me a savage look. A look that tried to get me up and going, though he didn't get much of a chance on account of my eyelids being swollen nearly shut. I mumbled nonsense back. Pa stuck the water spout in my mouth and washed out the gunky spit while I tried swallowing. Next thing I knew, Pa was spinning me around again to face Jerry. Seventeen years old, Jerry had his red towel draped over his giant head and the coach was kneading his shoulders, looking at us from his corner all smug.

Pa lowered his head to my ear. You win this or you don't eat tonight.

Then he slapped me on the rump and I stumbled from my corner like a drunkard, swinging aimless, Jerry coming at me. The stride of a champion. A mad moment thinking I could just fall to the floor and play dead, then the bastard would have a good sniff and leave me alone ... *Hey Pa, look, a new boxing move ...* but the moment passed as soon as it arrived 'cuz out of nowhere my opponent punched me in the gut as close as close could get to just below the belt.

Referee Rob's whistle. Above board!

Sounded like *all aboard.* Wished it was. Could have sailed right on out of there. Referee turned Captain. But Rob turned no such thing and Jerry grunted and nodded and came at me again though next time slower. Drawing it out, enjoying the kill. I was still bent double by the last punch so I staggered to his left without raising my head. Jerry was a couple feet away but next thing I knew, my feet were falling over each other and my body was flopping to the floor and I was gasping like a caught fish as the referee hopped it to me, wagging his finger over my gaping face.

One …

I tried telling Rob it was my feet not my head that went and tripped me up but he wasn't hearing none of it.

Two.

My mouth kept blowing bubbles.

Three.

I was falling again. Down through the ring floor, through the Earth to its goddamn core. The cold felt nice.

Four. Five.

Be done with it, then.

Six. Seven.

But then Jerry stomped over and just as I raised my head to give him a congratulatory thumbs up, he did something real stupid. Made a grinding motion with his jaw and spat on my shoes. A big brown wad of gob on my butcher-white clean shoes. Flames went up within me.

Eight.

I was on my knees.

Nine.

I was upright.

Rob grabbed my wrist and looked into my pupils, then nodded slight and stepped back. Jerry chuckled, pacing around me, wearing a sleazy smirk. I kept my breathing steady, my feet in one spot, waiting for the bull to charge.

When he did, I used his force and my right hand at the right time at just the right gap between his jabbing horns. Hooked my fist dead-center under his big fat dripping chin, hitting his sweet spot and then some. Jerry eyes lit up. Shocked, dazed, done. Deadweight log timbered to the floor.

Then it was his turn to be wagged at. I gazed from Jerry, unconscious, to the crowd, crazed, to Pa, who was whooping and bouncing me under my armpits like a newborn babe.

But I didn't care about any of that. About the cheering and the celebrating and being treated like I meant something. All I thought about was how, for the first time ever, my stomach would have something to chew on afterwards.

*

The rustle's clear gone by the time I get past that memory and to the bush. Bud's sniffing around, but all that gets us is a dead robin lying on its back with its claws clenching the air and its belly popcorning flies.

Walking on, we pass more bushes toward a running stream yonder, clear enough to drink from. I place each foot in front of the other, tentative. The ground's turning softer and spongier all the way up to the edge of the stream. I get on my knees and drink up. Bud also. Then I spot an apple tree. Apple trees are rare in these parts. The droughts over recent years haven't helped much, either. I tread over and touch it, expecting the bark to be made of mush and my hand to pulp right through. All deserts have mirages. Yet it's solid like a tree and smells like a tree, so I wrap my fingers around a low-hung apple and then I do get mush.

Rotten, the lot of 'em. With an exasperated cry, I turn 'round and slide my back down the trunk. Feels reassuring to have something to lean against. My hands drop to the ground, my legs stretch out like an Allen key. I'm trusting this tree's got roots running deep, holding it up strong, since all my strength's draining clear out of me.

Then hunger hits bad, and just as I'm thinking it, my head cracks open. Jesus H. Christ. If I wasn't dead before, I am now. My hand shoots to my temples expecting a spill of brains. I blink, not wanting to see the guck, and anyway my vision's distracted by something rolling away and I freeze for a second certain that the something is my head, but I'm clenching my own and I'm looking at an apple. This one perfect and ripe. A few others dangling in my periphery, high up and clear out of reach.

I grab the fruit before it rolls into the ditch then wipe the grime away, expecting the green to wipe off along with it or near as strange, but the skin stays green and even tastes like an apple. I spit the first bite out in any case, making sure it doesn't have worms of the dead wriggling 'round. Surprised when the flesh inside is tinged with the usual clean-green, so I chomp it down.

The meaning ain't lost on me, though—the eating of this apple. If this here tree is the Tree of Knowledge, then, screw me, I don't want any more knowledge what-so-fucking-ever. Am I doomed now? And how can I be when I'm doomed already and where's that snake and where the hell's God for that matter 'cuz he ain't warned me about nothing. Sitting quiet now, waiting for poison to fill my veins and the sky to fall down further or some such terribleness, something even more disastrous than what's already happened, but the only thing causing any fuss is my grumbling stomach wanting more.

I rise up, walk another twenty yards and I'm in the ghost of an orchard. Peach trees and apple trees and pear, too. A big beauty of an old apple tree catches my attention straight off. One that can just about house a man and his dog. There's a carved-out hollow in the decaying trunk surrounded by mushrooms—the non-poisonous kind—and an overflowing but manageable brook, plus an overhanging rooftop of branches connecting with a decaying peach tree. I pick a bunch of mushrooms and down 'em. The setting's just short of paradise as far as I'm concerned. Long moments pass, and maybe I've officially gone mad, and maybe I got those mushrooms wrong, but I hear a beckoning sound in the wind, coming from the tree, calling us over to take shelter and eat its offerings.

I get to its base and start collecting more goods. Bud circles 'round, yapping like a wannabe banshee, pawing and licking my fingers like I've got a three-course meal growing on 'em.

Shoo.

I bat him away and scour the ground, thinking there must be something good and smelly down there as that's where my hands are resting. Yet there ain't nothing close by except dirt and slimy things, like the soil's wormed everybody up and gone stirring them about the place.

You want one of these? Is that what you want? I ask him, sticking a mushroom near his nose.

He stops licking and whines and tilts his head to the sky. I crank my head and almost fall backwards. A creature is hung over a droopy branch like a disemboweled organ. Looks fresh enough to cook on a fire.

Protein. That's what I keep telling myself. I need protein and that's what I eat all the time. I pat Bud's head, assuring us both, and start preparing the ground with some sticks from the dry innards of the tree, then grab a few matches and the jackknife from my pocket. Despite the dampness in the air and all around, the fire springs up easy. I kiss the matchbox and stuff it back in my inner pocket.

It's the simple things that keep you alive, my friend, I tell him, plus whoever might be hearing. All a man's gotta do is think a little, pocket some essentials, and keep the fuck going.

Bud's almost treading on my feet he's so curious. I instruct him to scoot and lower myself on my haunches, lifting the squirrel's head to scan her some more. Everything's intact save for a few scratches running up her hind-legs. Her eyes are open, but then again squirrels don't blink much on account they're always watching for danger. My belly's growling big time. Still, I can't help staring into those wet jets for a few moments. Into all that observing brightness.

Feels like she's still in there looking out at the world somehow, I tell Bud soft.

He's ogling the critter like he can't believe she's up close. Chases after them something silly. Paws the tree trunks, yaps as his prey spirals clear from dog-shot, every single time. Must be strange for him, 'cuz it is for me, handling this one as though we're at a petting zoo. Shouldn't be allowed to do this. It's like we're cheating, trespassing on some ancient game, breaking the rules.

Squirrels always get away.

In any case, Bud's got dreadlocks of drool dangling from his chin, thinking of more practical things, so I place the creature back on the branch and tell him to settle down while I think things through. Don't know if I can go through with it, but I start preparing the tools anyhow. First dip my jackknife into the flames to sterilize it, then walk over to the brook and fill a dug-out knob of branch with clear enough water. I turn back to the fire. I hate doing the skinning thing and only tried it once when Pa forced me to, but now I'm grateful for the knowing.

Skinning a squirrel is just the same as plucking a chicken, I tell myself. Gotta do it to get to the edible bits. I lift the creature down carefully from the tree and place her between my legs as a grip hold. Then I make a small cut just above her butt and pull the red-bush tail clear over her head, peeling the fur back. When I get to the front, when the fur's all off and she's as naked as daylight, I notice bulges in her stomach. I brush my fingers over them. A thin slit across her abdomen and five babies come tumbling out, spilling onto the ground. Something splinters in me so deeply I almost can't bear to look. One eye squinting sees they're almost ripe. Tiny bodies, fully formed, waiting to greet the world.

Blind, deaf, and helpless, Pa would say if he saw 'em.

What did he know about animals anyhow?

*

Pa and me found Bud orphaned alongside the stream running to our farmstead. He was three, maybe four weeks old, a nub of a thing, which is maybe why he got left behind, though he was being kept company by a giant of a cat who was playing with him the way it would a mouse. Clawing and springing and deciding on what to do next. Pa told me to let the cat have him. Decided Bud was too worthless to even worry about. His little eyes looked cloudy, button nose almost torn off.

I returned to fetch him later when I was supposed to be chopping wood, finding the cat gone. Scooped him into my shirt and hid his shaky self in the shed, in some towels, plus a bit of hay with a tick-tock clock like I saw on some dog whispering show once, just to let him know there was a heart around. He survived mostly by keeping quiet. I introduced him to Ma and Pa when he was a stronger thing a few weeks later, after Pa spotted him chasing a butterfly around the duck pond. Ma smiled and gave him a little pat. Pa only shrugged, saying he didn't want anything to do with him, which I took as a yes to keeping him.

*

Anyhow, Bud springs forward like he still does with butterflies or anything buzzy, his black nose prodding the brown baby bulbs, sniffing their iron-rich world. Next second, he's glancing up like he's asking permission. He pushes one over, licks wary like he can't stand to chew it. He lets it alone.

Teeth clenched and mind clasped, I bury the babies by the tree, then toss my dog some de-furred skin and fat and other bits while I clear the creature out. I wash her insides and tie her squishy paws with a few leaf stems, then skewer her with a thick stick. Then I stare at the sky, mostly, while I heat the body over the fading flames. The clouds have cleared up some and the rain has reduced itself to the end of a long piss-dribble. Sky Station's still hiding, but whatever else is hanging around up there looks a little less ugly, which is a little more consoling. Some peachy light's been thrown in so it must be sun-setting time. I hang my boots and socks on a nearby set of logs next to the fire.

When I tend to the squirrel next, she's overcooking, but I'd rather burnt than bloody. I take her off the spit and eat quietly, chewing slowly. Halfway through, I find myself offering a prayer to Ms. Squirrel on behalf of us both. Thanking her for her life. I reckon it's the first prayer I've ever made that truly means something.

A while later, Bud belches something foul and lays his head in my lap. I take a few small sips of water from the knob and wipe my face with my shirt, then carry Bud to the tree hollow. I lay my gun beside me, then place my head on one arm and spoon my reeking dog.

Maybe I say it in my dreams. Maybe I say it before I drift off to sleep. But the last thing that happens before the world turns dark is me decidin' something solid and speaking it aloud.

Bud, no matter what, I ain't never gonna eat ya.

Chapter Seven

I wake up with a start. A purple line of pre-dawn is scouring the inky darkness. Night's dreaming was full of nasties: cracks running down the sky, rivers soaring above ground, wild beasts running after me, me running after them.

Pa's voice screaming in my ears.

Ma's whispering through the shed. It's okay, son, come on out now.

I close my eyelids and listen to the trees talking, the birds greeting each other like nothing's gone wrong. Then I fall back asleep. When I wake up again, dawn's arriving and Bud's departing, growling behind the line of purple that's all a sudden focusing to a point and I'm staring at my gun that's staring at me and at the end of that, a girl glaring.

Don't move.

Like I can. She's got me jammed inside a tree trunk. Bud moves, though. He gets to her side in a flash and growls.

She jolts backwards, tripping to the side. Recovers quick and aims the gun wobbly, eyes darting between me and Bud.

Bud. Git back here now, I tell him firmly.

Bud blinks. Growls again. Pads back.

Stand up, the girl says, voice hoarse.

I squint at her. You just said don't move.

Get out of the tree.

Her dirt-pocked face scrunches and I lean forward, then crawl out and rise up, pinning Bud's weight between my thigh and the trunk.

What do you want? I ask.

She's staring at me, wide-eyed. I wrap my jacket tighter 'round my chest and breathe in the windless air, stale now, and cold from the night. She's porcelain pale, like someone's taken her off a shelf. Blonde hair, bordering white. Plum-colored scarf coiled around a thin neck.

She had the guts to steal my weapon but she's about to topple in a stiff breeze. Fragile ain't the word. Splintery, more like. Makes me want to go over and catch her before she breaks. Either that, or grab my gun and shoot her, which is looking more likely. She's not ten feet from me. The gun nine.

Leave me alone, she says. Quit following me.

Her pupils are sparking fear and something else. Something like rage. Not the type to ignite.

I hold steady. The evidence couldn't be more obvious if she tried. I tilt my head to the knife at the ready in her other hand. Silver blade. Bone handle.

You sure about that? I ask, cautious. 'Cuz I'd say you've been the one following me.

She flicks a glance downwards.

Was at that car first, she says stubborn.

I keep my voice calm. You took my backpack.

Her shoulders drop. I saw light in the church. I thought people were in there.

I ain't people to you?

Her lips draw a line. Bud's pushing at my legs but I keep him pinned.

You had this on you, she says.

She points my gun at my chest. I flinch and lean back against the tree.

Which you've just stolen, I say slow.

I hold out my hand, palm facing up. She doesn't budge.

I saw that coffin spin away when you docked, she says. You can have the rowboat. I'm going to walk from here on.

We stare at each other for a beat.

Do you have any clue what's happened?

She swallows hard.

Do you?

A chuckle burns. Does it look like it?

She lowers the gun.

Where are you walking to next? I ask her.

Home, she blurts, flicking her focus over my left shoulder. The safest route from here is by road.

A road, huh? I'll be damned.

What about you?

What about me?

Where are you going?

I cock my head. Anywhere *but* home.

Silence. I break first. Why'd you steal my gun?

Wildfire in her blue-as-jewels eyes. Because you stole my tree!

She shouts it so loud, birds scatter from the neighboring branches. Bud darts to the left and after them. When he dashes back, he starts wagging at the girl like he can't help himself.

The sight calms me enough to say it polite. People don't own trees.

Not polite enough. Her body twitches and she stamps her foot like a tantrum, yanks at the zip in her track pants, drops the knife in the pocket, then raises the gun with both hands, aiming it direct at my chest.

Leave, she snarls.

My palms are up.

Alright. Alright, I say.

Her grip is all wrong and she hasn't pulled the catch but she's still holding my gun and there's no way I'm leaving without my gun.

I'm sorry I took another one of your shelters. Okay? And I know it looks different, but I promise you, I haven't been following anything but my own shadow since chaos hit. Me and my dog will leave right now, but I need to get back what's mine.

She starts chewing her lip, unsure, glancing at Bud.

Look, I need my stuff back, I continue. I've been pulling myself through this same as you, and I'd have probably done the same things you did if I kept bumping into me all the time, but now we have to move on. You tried helping with that bison. You wouldn't have done that if you wanted me clear gone.

Her glower's impressive.

I was worried for your dog.

I step forward. You don't trust people much, do ya?

Stop right there, she says, pupils alight.

Seven feet.

I'll shoot. I will.

Six. She's smaller the closer I step.

Five. My heart's pumping and I can tell hers is, too.

Four feet, stares holding.

She's not going to shoot. Something about her tells me so. Something behind that glare is so shot and sad, I'm not sure I can keep walking up to that kind of sad. Not now. Not maybe ever.

A ragged sigh and she lowers the weapon like it's a weight too heavy to hold. I reach out. A tremor of a pause and she hands it over. I pocket the gun. Her body's rigid but her breathing evens. An arrow of a look and she zips the pocket shut over her knife.

So. All good? I ask.

Silence.

Well, then.

I turn to go, motioning Bud to follow. He lags back, sniffing at last night's fire, at the tiny volcanos glinting in the ash.

Come, Buddy, I call. Time to shove.

Wait.

I turn 'round and she makes her way toward a pint-sized peach tree. Starts searching for something behind the stubby trunk. I keep a close watch while she gathers something in her arms and walks over, sheepish.

Here, she says, handing my backpack over.

I shoot her a look, then take the straps and hook them over my shoulders. The bag's a couple of jars lighter in weight.

Next time you want something, just ask for it, I tell her.

She hangs her head, says nothing.

Well, then.

I start walking.

Hey. The rowboat's the other way.

I'm not going back to that river until it gets easier to see through, I muffle over my shoulder. I keep walking in the direction where I'm guessing the road is, treading softly, listening for either footsteps or a pocket unzipping.

After a few seconds, footsteps. I exhale easier.

One condition, she says at my back. You walk in front of me the whole time.

I turn around. Offer a smirk. Thought we might be heading the same way.

Which way is that? she asks.

East. To Eashing. Then the coast after that. You?

She hesitates, then divulges. Close to Shackle Hill.

I know Shackle.

Her face turns ashen.

I hope they made it, she says quiet. You all alone, too?

My turn to hesitate. I got Bud.

I glance at our surrounds. What were you doing so far afield? I ask her.

Was walking, she says. Foraging, mainly. The sky was closing in so I thought to stay put in the forest and use the trees for cover.

She flinches a little.

You got *any* idea why all this flooding, and the quake?

Nope, I say. And there's no guessing how far this mess has traveled, no wristpod on me. Electricity's probably down for miles anyway.

She wraps her arms around her waist.

Wristpod?

I cock my head. Don't you own one? Thought all homes owned at least one. To link with Sky Station?

I need to get back, she says, blushing. The road's just over there.

I look where she's looking, slightly left of us, at the fields as tattered as yesterday, though the weather's settled down to a slow burn. Wind's gone and there's actually some sky up there—the charcoal dawn now kindling blues, tinged with gold. I turn toward the tinge. On a regular day, the rising sun would be a regular sun, but this morning, after three days of looking through a tunnel, it's like someone's shining a bright torch in my eyes. Tears start collecting at their edges. This could be my world after all.

Looks like we have ourselves an east, too, I tell her.

I step forward, thinking things through.

Wonder where that bison came from.

She's assessing me. I was going to ask you the same thing. I thought they didn't exist anymore.

They don't. At least not outside a fence. Must have escaped from the wildlife sanctuary about ten miles west of here.

She nods. I know of it.

I pull some peaches and mushrooms from my outer pockets. She declines.

You know, it's funny how things change based on how you look at them, I say, shrugging. When that bison was charging, I thought it was attacking. Maybe it was. But maybe it was running so vigorous because it wasn't caged up anymore. Maybe it was just running. Just happy to be free.

The girl considers me, quiet. I finish chewing a mushroom, then turn to go.

I hope this road you're talking about stays a road, I tell her over my shoulder. Though if we run out of pavement, we'll follow the sun as that's where Shackle's sitting and Eashing after that. There'll be help along the way, in any case. No way every farmstead's been bowled over by this violence.

She offers a mumble of something and keeps six steps behind, Bud trotting back and forth between. After a few yards, we get to the edge of the orchard where, lo and behold, there's a carved-out lane leading all the way to a fork, the left one heading in the general direction of town. Looks like the rain's either drained off the pavement or soaked right in.

Spirits lifting, I glance back at her. You haven't told me your name.

Eve.

I raise an eyebrow. Can't help but smile a touch. Now, that's a name for the times, I say.

Her pale cheeks redden. Yours?

I pause. Would you believe me if I told you it was Adam?

No, she smiles.

I turn back to the lane. Then you can call me Jack.

She says nothing about that, so we keep walking. A quarter-mile on, the path starts turning muddy and wet, as per. Yonder, there's a pond overflowing, rippling our way but harmless enough. Bud stops his trotting and treads alongside me like he usually does.

You know something, Buddy? I say in hushed tones. Last time I went to Eashing was with Frank. Took me to a kegger disguised as cards playing night. That was two Christmases ago, driving in his old clunker. We got there okay but had to tractor it back after the Chevy conked out near a mansion of a farmstead a mile or so from the bar. Frank convinced me the keys sitting in the front seat was a sign from God. Said the sprawling estate wouldn't miss it much amongst its other fine stock of equipment. When Pa saw us pulling in about 4:00 a.m. that morning, Frank was pointing a finger at my head and slurping that it was my doing. That he didn't know what had happened 'cuz he passed out somewhere between the last bar and my bad decision.

Well, that was the end of my treks to town. Pa wouldn't hear it how Frank was as drunk as a wine barrel and that I had to do something to get us back home. Pa even said that as my cousin was old enough to drink, he was old enough to *not* know what he was doing, but that I should have known better. Can you believe that crap? Grounded me for three weeks after that, but not before I was forced to return the equipment and work for the mayor for free. Turns out the thin green and yellow stripes painted along the tractor's side were the mayor's colors. How was I supposed to see colored paint in the dead of night?

I sigh. My dog's still looking up at me.

At least I got the chance to clock up some experience working for someone else, hey, Bud. Plus it got me out of the house.

I go quiet because Eve's footsteps have stopped squelching. I spin around.

She's gone.

My eyes open wide. Something's moving exactly where she's supposed to be following. Something slithering in the sludge, something almost swimming. In the quiet now, a slip of noise. Sinister, and sliding.

My lungs shudder. A cottonmouth is winding its way toward us. Saw one just like it last summer while fishing the Wren with Tommy. Olive body. Strange markings. At far enough range on the other side of the river to be freaked. This one at close enough range to be fucked. I grab my gun from my pocket, the scruff of Bud's neck, heaving him into my arms, bolting.

Then I trip up. Bad. Not thirty feet from where I just was. Splat hard on a dry piece of road that I'd give anything to be mud since my skull's ringing and my dog's squirming and I can't tell if it's because the

viper's got him or because the world's spinning, or because when I crank myself up and look back, all I see
is darkness and shadows and a world spinning darker
and I've been here before but usually in a boxing ring,
with ropes and a referee's whistle telling me it's over
and done with.

Chapter Eight

I'm smelling pork with potatoes. My nostrils soak it in.

Dinner's ready.

Betty's calling across two sets of doors, voice cheery and chirpy. I smile wide and lick my lips, tasting gravy laden with salt mixed with ... blood. My eyes crack open. Next thing I'm smelling is pork without the potatoes and Betty's voice fading to shreds and dead ahead, standing upright with barely a dent in the metal, letters and numbers winking in shards of light where the sun's hitting the metal and where the grit's not. A road sign: Eashing 5.5 miles.

First thought: I'm alive.

Second: Bud's alive, too. Panting heavy and hovering close, licking my bloodied leg.

I rise to my knees, head almost erupting.

Curving over and cradling my forehead in my fingers, I lick my palms where the blood's dry and salty, greedy for the iron. Feeling along my eyebrows, the right one tender and sticky. My eyelashes are caked.

Just hold on, I'm muttering to Bud, and to myself, since I'm shaking all over and remembering that snake that was probably just my mind playin' tricks since the sun's now high in a giddy sky, making everything bright and daydreamy. I look back and the sludge is still pooling, but nothing else is moving and nothing's bulging either.

Eve.

I squint through the glare, straining to see, straining to hear. Stillness strains back.

My gun's gone.

Fuck.

I peel my soggy backpack off. Surprised she didn't take this again, too, I mutter to Bud.

He offers a sloppy wag. Opening the main zip, everything is accounted for: underwear, shirt, photo of Pa. The weight of my jackknife is resting in my inner pocket. I take it out in any case and rotate it slow. I need to feel something tangible. Something real.

Doing a stock take of my busted body, my knees are scratched to high heaven, my left ankle's moaning, and my right elbow's numb. I clench the jackknife and stumble back down the pavement, groaning, eyes peeled for anything moving, humans included. After circling the sludgy road, too weary to panic, I slump down and gulp some water from a pothole, splashing it over my face and down my arms. Tastes like bad breath but I'll take it.

The metal sign is blinking at me. Calling me forth. I inhale deep. Gathering steam and sanity, I rise to my feet.

We've got to move on, I tell Bud. If you spot her

again, do me a favor and bark for once? Gives me a better chance to save both our butts.

Releasing a handful of mushrooms from the smaller front zip of my backpack, I swallow them whole while Bud pads to the sign. I watch as he gives the rusty pole a sniff before saluting it with a long piss. Then he takes off down the left fork, sniffing the bushes. Beyond the pond, Shackle Hill looms. A gradual incline doming the horizon. I follow my dog, forehead moaning and belly gurgling.

Okay, Bud, I'm coming. Just wait up, will ya?

He turns 'round and I catch up and we pad together, getting closer to the hill that's growing bigger all the while. Shackle's higher than Hawk and one I've never had the inclination to ascend. Wind's always blowing this side of the village and I use walking for walking, not for sightseeing, though at this particular juncture, climbing up and over will cut out a lot of road and a lot of what might not be.

We tread on for a mile or so, the pavement holding up, just. The tar's speckled with potholes, each filled to the brim like Sunday stews. The base of the hill is on our left. I start treading toward. Bud turns and pricks his ears at me. Then he does something stranger—rushes ahead, stops, then rushes ahead like he's seeing something but not sure he's wanting to see it. Or maybe he's hearing something because he's titling his head before rushing and stopping and circling again.

He's smelled or spotted or heard the girl. Must be. My muscles go on full alert. I crouch, but then

I hear it, too. A choir of churchy voices. Singing low and mournful. I take a few steps forward, standing on my toes, and spot an old water tower up on Shackle's summit. It's glinting in the sun, stuck next to what looks to be a small barn. Most of the trees up there are near enough flattened, so the sight is fairly clear.

I quicken my steps, my boots sucking the ground like they don't want to leave it, all the while gazing at the toy castle in the distance, for a moment thinking of Betty's centerpiece candle, but those ain't rabbits and they ain't sleeping. There's a barn there, and people in that there barn.

The singing's more distinct now. Women's voices and men's voices. Not many, but enough to keep me climbing, and the more we do the more I'm seeing life come back to life. Grass is visible, though it's more or less pulped green slime. Bud pauses to chew on a patch of longer blades.

You always puke that stuff up, I warn him.

He goes on chewing and I go on climbing, adrenaline and wind pumping equal measure. We're almost at the summit and the trees are thinning and making the path easier to follow, and I should be ecstatic at hearing other folks alive, and surely that means food, but I'm slowing down. The weirdest feeling. It's all those churchy sounds, making me magnet push-pull toward another magnet. Attracting, repelling. Repelling, attracting. I shudder at what's getting closer. What I'm getting closer to. Feels like a pulsing shadow, and I can't help stepping toward that pulse.

That being-followed feeling? I figured it was all gone after I met Eve. Now it's filling up the core of me and any second spilling over and drowning me in its flood. I topple over just with the thought. My hands clasp my knees. My knees clasp the earth. My lips and nose clog with spit, then a lick from Bud's drippy tongue sputters me out of my watery grave and back into the other one.

Blarhh.

I wipe my lips and raise my head to a wagging tail and another tongue-swipe along my chin.

Quit, alright?

I breathe deep and stand up.

I've had panic attacks before, but that was some-thing else. I hold my belly with my arms. The pulsing is beating right through me. Drumming me forward. Yep. It's that damn singing that's driving me nuts, my body its tuning fork. The hymns are bouncing off the trees. My nerves are twisting and the hymning's doing my head in.

I look at Bud, then ask the question, Race ya back down the hill?

But my dog's smiling and wagging like everything's fine.

You don't know what we're up against here, do you, Buddy?

More smiling and wagging.

Fine, I tell him. Have it your way.

We start zig-zagging over the fallen trees, looking for clearer ground. The top of the hill's starting to look like a monk's head. Bald on top with a blunt rim of forest running 'round its perimeter. The songs are rippling across the grass, ruffling the hairs on my skin. My muscles are vibrating and my chest is pounding. No turning back now. A hundred yards to go and the summit is leveling out to the monk's crown the size of a football field, the barn at its center, made of wood, riddled with rot. Entrance, a rib arching over a door ajar. Dark wood. Walnut. Windows dotted along the side walls, small and square and open, reflecting blue and green and tangerine.

Louder now, that hymning. Can't quite make out the words but I never listened much anyway.

Aching to arrive. Despising the ache.

Eighty yards. Heart pumping in my ribs.

Fifty yards. In my toes.

Twenty. My hands.

Could throw a football clear off this summit with all the tension in my body. Then the singing halts, my heart along with it. My ears strain against the quiet until a voice drones forth from deep within the barn's bowels. A preacher's voice. Fervent and foreboding.

Oh Father, in You we trust. For whatever has come to bear, whatever we have been delivered, we trust in You, oh Lord, to provide shelter, to nurture and provide. And if in the days ahead, we find no solace amongst ourselves, we find solace in You, oh Lord, for whatever You have delivered. For You have your ways of delivering that only You understand.

Quiet, again. I pull myself back from rushing, say

shhhtt to Bud to hold him steady. But of course he doesn't, just pads right up to the entrance, dressed in his smiley, Sunday best. I watch the tip of his nose, then tail, vanish behind the gap. A second later and I'm pressing the door open, my eyes adjusting to the dim, my mouth panting from the hike.

A few gasps as I bring in the light. A few more when they see what the light's brought in. Huge pulping pause when heads turn back to the preacher, who's standing at a makeshift haystack-on-end pulpit holding a Bible like a home-cooked pie, staring straight at me. He's tall and slim and leathery. I glance 'round the small spread of people, perched on a U-bend of wooden benches. The barn looks like any barn, just with more people and less animals—an upside-down Noah's Ark with its ribbed-hulled ceiling and flat-decked floor. I nod at the folk, shy, then spot Bud wagging at each one of them like a goddamn welcome wagon.

Preacher's still staring. His black preacher's robe looks two sizes too small.

I open my mouth to say something, but he opens his first.

Greetings, son. Take a seat.

Chapter Nine

The instruction's so simple and direct, I can't help but do as he says. I walk a few steps, relieved to be received, and sit down on an unused bench behind everyone else. About a dozen folks in all. No kids. No pets. Looks like they've met a shower in the last day or so, though the general appearance reeks of survival mode: worn clothes, shoes, expressions.

The preacher clears his throat and grips his Bible-pie as if to start up again, but then there's a shriek. A stout woman leaps up as Bud pukes near her feet. More or less pulped green slime. A few grimaces from the other folks while she staggers to the other end of the bench, snapping her head in my direction. Her face is plump and pink as a tomato, eyeglasses tilted. Scowls like I've just brought the garbage in. I give her a small shrug, tell Bud to come. He skittles over but lowers to the floor, slurping water from a crease in the stone, then pawing off the gunk glued to his whiskers. The woman realigns her glasses, walks over, and peers at the gash along my forehead.

Looks like you've been in a brawl, she announces.

Nothing more than usual, I mutter back.

A burning hush meets my burning blush as I look from the woman to the preacher to the rest of the congregation, all ogling.

Listen, I start. If anyone's got some information as to what's caused all this? Me and my dog have been camping out day and night since mayhem hit. We're heading to town. Had to leave home. It was ... broken up real bad and—

A bit more about what's caused this?

The tomato lady cuts in like I've stated the obvious.

The End of the World is what. And we're waiting for Jesus to save us.

She brushes her lashes up and down my dirt-speckled self.

But you sure ain't Jesus.

A stiff chuckle spreads through the space.

I'm Thelma, she says. And this is my barn. The horses have fled but we've got two milking cows, a sheep, and some chickens.

Thelma gives me another once over.

You got any fresh clothes in that backpack?

I nod while the preacher strides toward.

The sermon can wait, he says loud. Let's greet this brother as one of our own and see if we can't fill this here barn with some good will.

A wave of nods around the space. He opens his palm.

Samuel, he says.

I stick to Jack and he shakes my hand, then pats

Bud's head and leans a little closer. The man smells like old candles.

You must be hungry, son. Let's get you something to eat.

We shuffle 'round the benches, folks murmuring in our wake. A sinewy woman in pigtails and patched shirt interrupts our flow and hands me a damp cloth, plus a tin cup full of water. She motions to my head. The wound's dry, but I dab my skin with the cloth just the same, take huge gulps from the cup. The woman raises a thinner piece of dry cloth and leans forward to wrap it around my crown, but I tell her I'm good.

We have some large tubs and water jugs out back, she says. When you want, you can fill one and clean yourself up further.

I nod thanks and follow Samuel toward the back of the barn to a latch door. Tomato lady's following at a close distance. The sheep bleats as we pass. Samuel turns the handle and Bud skids past to an old storage closet turned kitchenette. Small and dark and musty.

We're having chicken in half an hour or so, on the fire, but for now this is what we got.

He walks over to the wooden countertop, lifts a pitcher, and pours some milk into a wooden mug. Then he pops open a large chest housing a key in its lock. Drops a handful of wafers into my palms.

I try looking like I hadn't retched them yesterday and place them on my tongue one at a time. Bud's at my feet drooling like a waterfall so I throw him a couple, then gulp the milk and ask for a top up for

Bud. The preacher obliges. He sure is tall. And thin as these wafers. Wouldn't last long in a fight but at least he'd see the man coming. I glance at the door and the people flocked behind it.

I keep my voice dim.

That lady saying it's the End of the World. She's kidding, right?

Samuel narrows his eyes at me. Not sure if that's a good sign or a bad one.

How'd you find us, son?

I spotted the barn from the road. The fork leading from the orchard? All those trees blown aside like that. Anyways, we were making our way east toward town when I heard the singing. Folks have been few and far between since all that madness with the earthquake and such.

Samuel stares at me. I gulp a breath down.

Surely, this natural disaster's been a local thing? Glad to have found you folks along the way, in any case. Finding food and cover's been such a bitch. Sorry, Father. Anyhow, my dog and I would appreciate some shelter for the night, then we'll be on our way come morning. Town yonder wouldn't have been hit that bad, surely.

Samuel's stare turns curious.

Now, why would you think that?

About the disaster being local?

No, about you thinking it's natural.

I pause, wondering how to put it.

Because something this ugly would only happen to

a shit-small—sorry, Father—outpost like Overstraddle and surrounds. What'd we have to lose in these parts? Weather's always doing funny stuff in this valley, besides. Sounds crazy, I know, given this much destruction, but I suppose the thought's been keeping my feet moving ... that no doubt what's beyond this valley has held up better. You know? Even if that earthquake or whatever the heck it was traveled that far across, surely ... I trail off.

Samuel's squinting as though there's grit in his eyes. Then he closes his eyelids and starts twining his fingers around a large wooden cross hanging on some string around his neck. I glance out the window again.

You saying all this is a supernatural occurrence? I ask him.

His eyes snap open.

How about we take a trip up the water tower, he says. Then you can see the extent of the situation for yourself. You got enough energy for that?

I nod, and he waves to the door and leads me out the back of the barn, past Thelma and a couple others looking, toward the water tower posted on the north side. Bud at my heels, I tell him to sit still while the man takes off his robe and starts climbing the ladder, which looks a century old and too busted to be climbing. He's wearing blue jeans and a black T-shirt. Some ancient rock group printed on the front. I strip my backpack and place it by Bud.

Watch the sixth step, Samuel calls over his shoulder. It's loose.

I ain't used to heights. I follow behind, hands and boots gripping the bars. Samuel arrives near the top in no time, sending a pigeon flapping straight past my neck. A soft cooing from somewhere close and another pigeon's nesting in one of the cross-sections of metal about halfway up.

I get to the top and make a point of not looking down. Feel woozy just thinking about it. Quick glance at the preacher and he's watching the sweat dripping from my chin. I wipe it away and inhale sharp and open my eyes. My teeth almost fall out. Can see Eashing as well as the lake framing it in the furthest distance. Can see lots of things. Problem is, in every direction, it's the same scene. Buildings collapsed like piles of matchsticks. Water where it's not supposed to be, covering everything. Cars tipping in it. And no humans. Not a single person or animal in sight. I hang my head, sighing heavy at what's below as well as what's staring me right in the face.

Yeah, well, we don't know what's past all this though, do we?

I sound as desperate as a fish, gasping on the chopping block. And something's gasping inside me, alright.

Samuel considers me. Makes his voice somber again.

I'm afraid we do, son. God has spoken and spoken true. The world has ended and we must wait for His good grace for it to begin again.

He dips his head, brings his palms together, then

looks up at me under a fringe of black hair. I squint at him. Something about his clothes and manner ain't sitting right.

I cock my head.

You even a preacher?

He smirks.

I preach, don't I?

We meet eyes.

What's going on, *Father?* I need some answers real soon about what's happening. I need to know if ... if there's a chance of having a life out there.

Feel so awkward saying it, I can't meet his gaze. Instead, I look up. Clouds are gathering, stitching white with gray.

Samuel strokes his jaw, then stretches his arms.

Okay, he says direct. You know it's a good thing, what you're asking. It's a good thing. Better you keep questioning. 'Cuz once you got no more questions then you got all the answers, and if you think you got all the answers, then you're missing the biggest question of all.

I raise my eyebrows.

And what question's that?

Whichever one comes next.

Samuel's lips curve and his fingers tuck into his jeans. Eyes clamped on me, he draws a cigarette and lighter. Spurs the wheel and a tiny bonfire sparks. He takes deep drags. After a minute, he offers the butt's burning entrails. I decline.

Call it a flood or *the* Flood, he says, but the water's

still rising. Sooner or later the waves might even rise up this here hill. And we gotta be ready. Seems like something wants to wipe us all out and Hell, it's likely nature's doing the overtaking, but the congregation believe it's something a little more biblical than that and they need to keep believing it.

I narrow my eyes.

How come?

The man rubs his hands like they're cold.

Belief won't get you far. You gotta know something to know it. Having an opinion on things ain't nothing but thoughts swimming around each other, sucking on each other's scales. There ain't nowhere or nothing beyond those scales. Nowhere to surface. Only swimming and circling till you don't know if you're coming or going. A big fucking ocean of unknowing. Belief, son, is one shot blind of ignorant. One shot closer to looking up your own asshole.

He tips his head to mine and places a finger to his lips.

I stopped sucking a long time ago. But these folk? They still gotta believe 'cuz they've always done so and it makes them feel safe. Keeps them from asking questions. You should have seen these people when the shit hit. You'd think they'd have been the calmest of the lot, but no. Most everyone was "Hell Marys," not "Hail Marys," and well, I had to do something. Had to ease their minds and remind them of what they'd always believed—that this is God's doing, that the End has come. That this here's the Devil's time *being* up, not him *showing* up. Had to do that or else they would have wiped each other out the day they almost were. Fear and panic are beasts, sometimes even more so than seeing blind.

The man clocks my confusion and pauses his diatribe.

You getting me? He asks.

I gaze at the sodden view for a few moments.

You're saying you want them to believe in the End of the World so that they feel less panicked than if they knew there were truer reasons, like a natural disaster or somethin'?

He clicks his tongue, smiles wide.

Yep. Father had been the preacher in this here village for years. He was in the clergy house when it all went down. Died when the roof caved in. I was at the chapel next door babysitting and had to take over. Never wanted the burden, I can assure you. But these people were looking to me for guidance as though it was in my genes or something. Do you know half of them died before they even got to the chapel? And most who did are near enough to occupying their grave allocations already. Still, someone's got to take charge. Someone's gotta keep doing something other than just believing. That's true surviving.

I rake my fingers through my hair.

He smiles again.

Listen, son. My gut says it's the weather, and my gut's usually right. Storms and quakes. Bad ones, sure, but nothing apocalyptic. Unless that something apocalyptic is affecting the weather. But if it's keeping these folks in line, I'll keep saying it's God as long as I have to. There's been no satellite contact or anything letting us know for sure, so I've taken it as my responsibility to hold fort. For now. At least until emergency services come our way. The flooding's gotta stop at some point.

He follows my gaze to his bare wrists.

We don't use wristpods in these parts. Father stored one, but he rarely used it, far as I knew. Any case, it went down same time as the roof and Father did. God's the only protection we need, got me?

My shoulders drop.

So you've had no communication with Sky Station either, I say somber.

He shrugs, sniffs the air.

Good thing Thelma has been able to house this many, though survivors have been few since that first day. No one except you has come for days.

The man glances over my shoulder, then slumps down on the landing, legs dangling, and lights another cigarette.

I just hope that woman keeps her head on. Folks are starting to get nervy and she's been the worst of the lot. You know how religious people can get even more crazy religious? Fire and brimstone mentality. You say you've travelled from Overstraddle?

I look west to where he's looking. My village is lying in tatters. Shreds more like. The crater, a deep cut in the earth's skin, stretching post to post to Cattle

Village. The farmlands, blackened birthmarks. River Wren, a wide-open wound still oozing brown. The vision's so vile, I almost don't hear what the preacher says next, something about a girl missing, but when it filters through, my muscles curl.

A girl, you say?

He nods.

Sixteen. Full of surprises, that one. Eve's always going off into the woods, gathering herbs and such. Has a way with plants, animals, all things nature. One of them fairy types. Anyways, she went wandering that day. I thought maybe you'd come across her. Anyhow.

What do I mention first? The stalking, the knife, or the gun?

I shake my head and he hangs his. I try sounding neutral. She your daughter or something?

Sister. Adopted, he says. Father found her in the orchard on one of his morning walks before sermon. Someone had left her in a big old apple tree. She was six, maybe seven months old.

An apple tree?

Yeah. Snuggled in the hollow.

I swallow hard.

Aunt Bethany took care of her, mostly, until Bethany got married and had kids of her own. I was about Eve's age now, actually, when we took her on.

He shakes his head.

I told her she'd get into trouble one day, always going into those woods alone. And now look. She's walked straight into the wild gone more so.

Coils of cigarette smoke snake past my neck. I chance a glance down and check on Bud. He's sleeping sound. A pigeon lands close to us, curious.

Samuel continues his musings. Did you know the daily nourishment for pigeons is seeds, grains, berries, that sort of thing? Only wild pigeons will sometimes eat snails and worms and such. Now, that's a question for you. How do these little creatures adapt from living in a civilized world to a savage one overnight? Where they gonna find fresh grains? Where they gonna get their berries?

Samuel takes a last inhale. He stubs his cigarette on the metal and flings the butt past my shoulders. I stare at him.

It ain't littering if the world's an ashtray, he says, shrugging.

I glance at the barn.

The congregation. You mention anything about emergency services coming?

He grimaces. Wouldn't want to get their hopes up just yet. Hope dropped is worse than any raised. At least for their kind. Hope ain't a thing sitting on a shelf waiting to be dusted. It's being able to fly off that shelf knowing it's got wings and trusting they'll fly to something better. Anyways, whenever rescue happens, these folks can start poking around someone else's pulpit.

He sighs and motions us down the ladder. I descend first, reaching the water tower's base wiped and daunted. Then I spot smoke of a different sort hurling upwards on the other side of the barn. Fumes laced with chicken fat. Bud's woken up and he's already turning the corner, nose leading the way. I tug on my backpack.

We got berries for now, I mumble.

Samuel pulls his arms through the sleeves of his robe, the cuffs landing at his elbows, the bottom hem brushing his knees.

Yep, Samuel says. For now, we got berries.

Chapter Ten

Chicken's never tasted so good.

I try chewing in small bites, but end up gulping the meat down same as Bud.

Chugging back a gallon of water, I hear a commotion increasing in pitch on the other side of the barn. Samuel pricks his ears and drops his empty plate, shooting straight past me. Bud also. I follow both. At the top of the hill, the congregation is doing just that—congregating around someone who I can't see, but who I'm guessing it must be. Bud's guessing, too. Finds his way easy through the maze of legs, parting the crowd, and I'm staring at a girl with angel hair and fiery eyes who's staring at me as she would death, as she would a nightmare come 'round again.

We lock eyes, then blink away. The crowd doesn't notice. Bud pads back and I pat him quiet. A buzzing of chatter and people swirling 'round, a horse blanket thrown around Eve's shoulders. Her scarf is missing. Samuel places his hands on her elbows, steadying. Thelma gets close and gasps. She calls for cloths, then brandy.

I step closer and there's a bloom of pink flowering on Eve's forearm, near her wrist. Samuel rolls up the fabric of her shirt and she winces. The flesh is marked by a double rainbow of red dots.

If she was pale before, now she's completely washed out, drained of all color except the patterning on her skin. Samuel guides her through the entrance of the barn, talking low in her ear. A few folks are still gathering around the leftovers at the fire, but most follow inside. Samuel tries lowering the girl on the bed of hay but she resists and sits down instead, tucking her head in the crook of his bony shoulder.

She's sniffling and her knees are touching. Her arms go to her belly, swaddling. Thelma bends over and points in a hurry around the barn like she's showing it to the girl for the first time. Eve sweeps her eyes past me. I've taken position two stalls down, standing next to the pen housing the sheep, though Bud's in center stage, wagging docile near her feet. I wonder if I should ask for my gun now, or wait till she offers it back. Then I remember what I told Samuel. More, what I hadn't told him. I say nothing, and stay put.

The pigtailed and patched shirt woman saddles up and hands Thelma a brandy bottle. Thelma grabs it, opens the cap, takes a big swig.

Thanks, Joan, she says, then scours Eve's arm. The girl winces again.

Samuel, that there's a snake bite. Look at the puncture marks.

A few gasps from the crowd as Samuel leans in and

Eve nods, tears streaking down smudged cheeks. I swallow tight. Eve mumbles something and Thelma shakes her head.

Looks venomous to me, the woman says. Here.

She offers the brandy bottle but Eve turns her chin.

You been conscious this whole time? Thelma asks.

Eve nods.

Breathing okay?

Eve nods again.

Hmmm. Still. We need something small that's sharp enough to cut with. Anyone got something sharp?

I hold my tongue, but my hand's in my pocket now, gripping my jackknife. Eve glances sideways. I might be mistaken, but I think her head's shaking at me real slow.

Let's not do anything rash, the preacher says. She's doing alright.

Look at her, Samuel. She's pale as milk. When'd you get bitten, girl?

This morning, Eve croaks. On my way past the orchard.

Thelma looks up to the ceiling, hands on her hips.

Still, she says. You should lie down.

Thelma's face scrunches and her hand clamps her mouth as though something's just come to her.

This is a sign that the Devil's at work, is what this is! That snake and her name combined! And with those ominous clouds gathering outside again!

The woman falls to her knees.

Jesus, save us now, she moans, dipping her forehead. This child is back in our fold but with a sign that all's not well. All's not well!

Samuel purses his lips. Exhales slow.

Now's not the time for jumping to conclusions, Thelma. We have to trust in God's plan and we have to think practical, too. Eve's doing alright. Seems a dry bite.

As he says it, Joan returns with a mug of milk and few strips of chicken, plus a warm smile. Her mousy hair's tied up, but a few strands are dangling near the milk. Eve ignores the chicken and reaches for the milk. She takes a big swallow. Thelma stands up, her face turning a riper shade of tomato.

I'm one of the most practical people around. You know that. And that means doing something. We need to cut that poison out before it infects the rest of—

Enough! Samuel releases Eve and stands up and over the woman. We've all been seeing things a little skew. Situation's tense enough under the current circumstances—

It's been three days, preacher. Three days, and patience is running thin.

Samuel stays mute and Thelma scowls, lips drawing in.

Fine, she says. Have it your way. Eve's in your hands now. And those hands better pray hard.

Thelma stomps toward the front of the barn, motioning for the congregation to follow.

They hover, expressions alarmed. A minute more and they disperse in packs, leaving me and Bud in plain sight.

I scan the barn. The closest exit is the one Thelma and the others have just departed from. If I go out that door, it will seem I've joined ship, which feels more awkward than staying where I am. Eve's turned her gaze toward the back of the stall anyhow, knees in fetal position, fingers kneading the horse blanket.

Father?

Samuel shakes his head. Eve's face falls.

I saw how the clergy house was almost swept away, she says soft. The chapel ...

Samuel pats her hair.

We climbed up as soon as the kitchen began flooding. How'd you manage to stay safe?

I found shelter. Terrain got a bit easier the closer I traveled, but then the snake bit me. A viper, maybe, but I don't think the puncture went deep. Had to rest some, is all.

Eve pulls her wrist up to view, stares at the wound.

Don't mind Thelma, alright? Samuel says. Everyone's a little on edge just now. Just stay close.

She looks at him.

Where's there to go?

Eve raises the mug as Bud shuffles over, asking please with a paw on her knee. She gives him a small pat.

Who's this?

My throat clinches. Samuel glances over his shoulder.

Dog arrived with this fellow earlier. Jack, do you mind giving us some space here?

Sure thing, I say, neutral as possible. Come on, Bud.

I step closer and grab my dog by the neck.

Come, Buddy. Let's go wash up.

Eve's avoiding eye contact, and seeing nothing weighting her pockets, I walk away. I'm almost at the door when I hear her voice raising a little louder than it needs to.

Everyone I came across was dead, Samuel. Either dead, or dying in front of my eyes.

Chapter Eleven

Clouds breaking. Thunder ripping. Night's rolling in, full of thorns and lashings, and we're crouching in the barn that's creaking like a boat, all the animals crouching, too. Samuel goes to the window, rain beating against it.

Won't be long now before the storm passes, he says confident. Storm's breaking over there.

Thelma stomps up to his side and pushes her way to the window, then stares at him cold.

That's only the full moon doing funny tricks with the light, she says. That's not breaking nothing.

She walks over to Joan, wraps her arms around her shoulders, and guides her back to their stall. The others are either dozing or wrapping their knees in their arms or bringing their fingers to prayer. Eve's sleeping sound and Bud also.

I get up, chest tight.

Samuel? Can I have a word?

He's still standing by the window and I don't think he's heard me through the din of the storm. There's a diving whoosh, followed by a loud thud. Samuel and

I lean our heads on the glass, and five feet yonder, a pigeon is lying on its side, neck slack, eyes cloudy. Its wings twitch once. Twice. We exchange glances.

Wonder when it's gonna stop, I ask him.

The storm?

I pause.

Yeah.

Someone taps me on the shoulder and I almost jab her with my elbow. It's Joan, standing real close. I can see her upper lip shaking.

You remind me of my own son, Matthew. Just shy of fifteen, he was. Tried saving me from the water, but a current got hold of him and took him clear away from—

She trails off, sucks in her breath.

Your family, she says next. You were with them when it happened?

I stare at the ground.

Yeah.

I'm so sorry, she says. Must've been awful.

The woman takes a tissue from her pocket and makes like she's going to hand it over but raises it to her temple instead.

Just awful, she says. How did you manage to survive, son?

I shrug. Guess surviving is what I do best.

A sweeping behind. The back door swings open, then bangs shut. Opens again like someone's exhaling but not quite since there's no one on the other side. It slams again. All eyes on the door and a mad gasp from

Thelma as it keeps swinging and slamming. Faster. Louder. I fight an urge to bolt through that gap and escape the barn entirely.

Bud does the bolting for me. Don't know what's come over him but he bursts through and starts barking. I fling myself out the door, punching it open as it swings back, and shout for him. At first, I can't see his shape for the rain, but then he circles toward and lifts his muzzle like he's drinking the drops. I'm soaked through already, arms arching over my head, peering.

What, Bud?

Then I hear it. Impossible in this weather, but there it is: an airplane. Single-seater. Small, swerving, and circling toward us.

Chapter Twelve

The engine is sputtering loud. I'm swinging my arms and Bud's going ballistic. Folks start spilling out of the barn, chickens running amok, tripping them up. A rumbling crash from behind and I move out of the way as Samuel rushes by and raises to his tiptoes, robe sleeves swinging at the plane that's curving back around, waggling its wings in greeting.

Samuel turns, spots me gawking, and grins wide. I nod back. Emergency services, it's gotta be.

Samuel rushes back to the barn while the plane levels and flies closer still. Shouts and whoops and silence as folks watch on, transfixed. A woman sprints past me, yelling a warning, though I don't know why until I see it for myself. The pilot's not slowing or smoothing for a landing but dipping and teetering the aircraft something harsh.

Then, screaming. The plane's shuddering. Shaving the water tower. Nosediving. I watch on, pinned, as the blades whip the barn roof right off. A thunderous explosion. The barn's swallowed the cockpit, bellows of fire licking, wings sticking out and tail sticking up.

Eve.

I rush past the fleeing cows and sheep toward the barn, burning bright now. The stench of melting metal is overwhelming.

Squinting through the toxic smoke, I see Samuel staggering across the threshold with a body in his arms. He halts just short of the downpour and leans against the wall. His robe is wrapped around the torso like a body bag. I tread over, the heat of the fire competing with the cold of the rain—a sizzling sweat.

Take her, he gasps. And take it out.

I stare at him, stumped. He lifts the robe and exposes Eve's forearm: hot red and swollen angry. He lets the fabric fall over the snake bite, his chest falling forwards, too. I catch Eve at the same time Samuel lurches to his knees, one arm steadying his weight on the grass, the other at his back, fingers grabbing his T-shirt for the piece of shrapnel stuck near his spine. Daggers are piercing his shoulders and bare neckline and there's scarlet dripping from his lower lip.

No.

I swing 'round. Everyone's dealing with their own personal apocalypse—shouting for help, sprinting to help, sobbing.

Samuel.

He holds up his hand.

Take—her, he wheezes, and falls face first to the ground.

I spin, looking for an exit. Through the raining smoke, side-stepping the falling debris, shouting for

Bud to follow. I stumble past the west wall where the nose of the cockpit is crushed beyond belief. A cracked helmet's just visible. The rest of the body not. Gazing up at the tail, glistening white in the licking flames, heat blasting my face, I'm looking for emergency colors and I don't see emergency colors. I see thin green and yellow tractor-type stripes. The mayor's plane. I curse loud. The guy wasn't trying to get in. He was trying to get out.

The silo.

Eve's eyes are fluttering at me. The black fabric raises a touch. She turns her head and blinks.

Silo, she utters again, pointing.

Against the charcoal horizon is a dark smudge, two hundred yards down slope. Small as a thumbnail. I carry us toward it, my dog a magnet behind. Arriving on its doorstep, I glance at the turmoil behind me, fire now roaring and rippling across the length of the barn, specks of people flickering about. I squeeze the raindrops from my eyes and launch us in, the door giving way to a vault, domed and empty, metal walls dented and shot with tiny holes. I lower Eve on the stone floor, dust flouring up. The space has hardly any light left, save for shafts of silver piercing the holes. But the shafts are so sharp, for a second, I'm convinced some alien ship has landed on the summit, about to take us all. Then I remember the harvest moon that was cresting just before the storm.

Then, another apparition. A black ghost hanging from a nail on the back of the door, its flesh almost touching mine. I leap over Eve and almost slam Bud against the wall, cursing from here to Kingdom come.

Bud cowering and me shaking, my eyes adjust to a priest's robe dangling and thudding the door. There's a lump in its front pocket. Heart still hopping, I step 'round the girl and glide my fingers into the fold, feeling the cold metal of my gun, plus her knife. Thank Christ. I pull them free, stash them at the back of the silo. Then I take the dry robe off the nail, replace it with the wet one covering Eve's body. I take the jackknife from my pocket, slice a long bandage from one of the robe's sleeves, then lower to my knees and raise her wrist. She's out for the count now, which is a good thing.

The blade's a few inches from her skin, ready to cut, though I haven't any sense how deep to go and if it's gonna do any good whatsoever because the venom would have traveled everywhere by now and do I even use a tourniquet and anyhow Eve's opening her eyes and staring at me, terrified.

I lower the jackknife.

I'm only helping, I tell her. The snake bite. It's swelling up bad.

She yanks her arm away from my grip and slides up against the wall, huddling.

You're burning up. Samuel told me to cut the venom out.

Where is he? she rasps.

She's sweating, hair dripping. The rain's beating sharply against the metal walls. Tears are streaming down her face. She lowers her head to her knees.

He's dead, isn't he?

Bud pads over and places his head near her feet.

I speak soft. We need to cut the venom out.

Leave me alone.

Her shoulders are heaving and she's lifting her head, staring at me. I move closer.

I can't do that.

I move closer still, but she pushes further back against the wall, sobbing.

Leave me alone!

Sobs tremble the air. Then everything goes motionless like a clock tripping up time. Eve starts collapsing and I steady her before she thumps head first to the floor. Her eyes are open, but they're swimming in the light.

The stars, she says, voice clear. So many.

She turns her gaze to mine. Her paleness is muted against the steel. Her blue eyes are dark and wide and watching like an owl's. Then she blinks like one. A slow draw of a blink. A shushing blink. A creature of the night, of all things seen and seeing.

You know what I've liked most about the world falling away?

I frown. Hold her tight.

The darkness that comes with the night. Seeing nothing but what's been here all along.

I look at her, dumbstruck.

The stars that shine through, she presses. Stars, and silence.

Then she closes her eyelids, goes limp and I'm holding her weight on my lap, worry cutting right through. If she was burning before, now she's on fire. Placing her gentle on the ground, I change out of my drenched clothes as quick as possible and take the dry robe off her body and throw it over my own so that she can cool and I can warm.

I'm breathing rapid. Breathing for us both.

I lean my back against the tin, trying my best to keep calm. Minutes go by—ten, a hundred—when the rain suddenly stops. Eve's limp, but still alive. I stand up slow, walk the few steps, open the silo door. Then I breathe in the night air and gaze at the sky turning light with one star, then a sprinkling, then an explosion. Sky Station gleams. Slumping to the ground, exhausted, I imagine lonely angels. Though the world is broken, I imagine lonely angels sending me off to a lonelier sleep, a sleep so deep it will wake me up in another place on another planet in another sky screaming the same beauty as this one.

*

Dawn's breaking. I'm walking from the shed toward my bedroom. When I open the door, Pa's sitting on my chair with his head in his hands. He doesn't look up.

Come here, he says.

His fingers are threading his hair.

I do as he says. He's got his pajamas on. The black ones. Black slippers. A thief in the night, only it's the beginning of a new day.

Come here.

More threading.

The bed's pinned up against the wall, exposing porno mags and Ma's handgun lodged between the planks. The desk lamp's lying on the floor, the lampshade hanging from its skeleton rim and the dislodged lightbulb cracked open and leaking rust on the cream carpet.

The curtains are pulled a little open. A dim light's misting the room, his bald spot smudged red like a stain. His fingers are making a web over it.

I swallow hard. I've walked from one crime scene into another and I ain't got a clue what I'll be charged with next: the magazine with the girls, the magazine with the boys, or the gun. My eyes skim over the magazines and the gun and land on the lightbulb.

I'm sorry I hit you, I say. I wasn't thinking clear. My head. All that hymning and chanting. All that listening. Look, Pa. I'll never ditch church again. Okay? Pa?

Come here.

I walk over and he raises his head and reaches out. I hold out my good hand. He doesn't shake it. I hold out my bad hand, and he wraps his fingers around mine, held tight in Ma's kerchief. It's the first time he's ever held something of me. His eyes burrow into mine. His fingers press into mine. Then he points to the gun.

You know what to do, is all he says, then leaves the bedroom.

Bud's sitting just outside the door, looking at me weird.

Git, I tell him. He whines a little.

Git, I tell him and I walk over and close the door on him.

Then I step toward my upturned bed for Ma's gun. My foot lands on something sharp. A shard of lightbulb is digging at my heel. I pluck it out, droplets falling. I lower to my knees and grab the lightbulb and break it further into yin and yang halves. Without another thought, I lay back and slice my left wrist. Pink flows and pain follows. Then I slice my right wrist with wobbly fingers.

After the shock of the slicing, a numbness grows. I wonder at that—how quickly life can spill out and blank you out. How merciful the body can be when you want done with it. And it's shutting down quick. The dizziness in my head. The pumping of my heart. Then, more faint, like a bygone watch ticking down its own battery. And I wonder at that too. How the heart can bleed when you ain't got the care or consciousness to give a shit about the stains.

And then he finds me, just before I melt away. Probably smelled the blood. As it blends with the rust of the lightbulb and the cream of the carpet, as my body and heart lay open and pulsing on the floor, the last thing I see is my dog padding over, sniffing the whole of me before lying near my chest.

Bud has found me again, so I pull him close.

Chapter Thirteen

Pain's compressing my muscles, stop-and-start spasms tweaking 'round sharp corners. I jerk upright and snap my eyes open from the nightmare. I stare at my wrists. They're as smooth as marble, though pricking hot. Rubbing my eyes, I check my wrists again. I've never cut them, not like that. I lean my head between the indents in the tin, staring at nothing, thinking of everything.

I check on Eve again. Her fever's broken and she's still breathing and it's still full-moon dark. I check the cottonmouth bite as I've been doing all night, in and out of ragged, jagged sleep. I think the swelling's gone down, but I can't be certain. Bud's sleeping calm near my legs. Rotating my shoulders, I'm about to doze off again when I hear a polite knocking on the door ajar.

Matthew? Is that you?

Joan's gawking at me.

It's Jack, I tell her cautious. I'm Jack.

Oh, she says, sweeping her long, thin fringe from her forehead. She blinks at me twice, then pats her chest softly. Looks at me for a long moment with big brown eyes. Well, most folks are dead, she continues. Thelma's praying. That fire ...

She stops talking and stares at me like she can't push any more words out. I get up and place my hand on her bony shoulder, peering over her head toward the barn. The sight is humps and holes. The smell, cindery sharp and smoky metal.

But I've come to tell you that we're doing okay and Jesus is on his way, she says, eyes brightening. That's why I've come. To tell you that Jesus is on his way.

I try to not roll my eyes as she turns on her heels, one shoe on, the other missing, teetering back over the small rise. Toward an outpost already turned relic.

I rub my forehead then sink down, aching, onto the dust-ridden floor, which sparks a round of coughing. My nose is clogged, my chest is racking, and I feel like I always do when I'm getting sick.

A murmur beside me. Eve's moving.

Hey. I reach out and check her pulse. Her eyelids flick open.

Jack?

I'm right here. You okay?

I'm starving, she moans.

I exhale.

Good, I tell her. Everything's back to normal.

Grabbing Samuel's robe from the nail, I swing it around her shoulders. It's still damp, but not as drenched as her clothes.

Change into this. It's summer and all, but you should wrap up.

I sit her up slow and she nods thanks. Then I turn away, sneezing loud into the black depths of my sleeve fold.

I'm going back to the barn. Need to check the extent of the damage and find us some food. Won't be long.

I step toward the door. Bud's already past me and slurping rainwater from a tipped pail. East is starting to wake up—a wash of honey, streaking wide. I stretch and spot another pail around the curve of the silo, this one upright and filled to the brim. I ask if she's done changing, and then heave the water into the small circle of space.

Here, you go. Enough to drink and wash with, too.

Eve wipes her mop of hair from her brow. Her forearm's still red.

You sure you're okay?

She shrugs. Jack?

Yeah?

Thanks.

Sure.

I mean it.

Sure.

We exchange glances.

Just be here when I get back, I tell her.

Chapter Fourteen

I almost laugh, the visual's so absurd. Thelma's crouched beside the water tower, milking a cow like a normal farm day. The woman's hunched over a plastic tub, arms piston-pumping the cow's teats, getting squirts, and when I walk closer, her red face is streaked with soot, both eyeglass lenses splintered, apron a charred piece of cloth.

Thelma?

I step closer.

Thelma?

I told you the Devil was playing tricks, she spits, eyes fixed on milking. I knew it. But you wouldn't listen. Only spouting words, you. No substance behind 'em.

She glances backwards at the ruins and shakes her head.

No wonder.

She licks the milk running down her forefinger, grabs the bottom of my robe to wipe her finger dry, almost yanks the whole thing off my naked self.

And that Eve. I'm telling you, Samuel, the Devil

came back with her. Look at this evildoing. The Devil is back!

I stay mute. The cow's grazing the patch of long grass growing at the base of the water tower. A runway of burned grass leads back to where the front door of the barn once stood, now a skeletal socket framing a hollow eye. Other patches and lumps of black and burnt are dotted 'round, patches and lumps my eyes ain't willing to focus upon. There's a box-sized section of barn still standing along the south corner, with a large candle quivering against the fractured pane of glass.

Does anyone need help? I ask, trying for neutral.

Thelma snorts. We all need help.

She wipes her brow and squints at me.

Speaking of, do something useful and go milk that cow over there. The rest of the folks are inside praying for the souls departed, and for Eve, now gone to the light, we hope. God bless her tarnished soul.

I look where she's looking and there is a cow yonder, close to the sheep and chickens grazing in a make-shift timber pen, but it's lying on its side, teats flowing something other than milk.

I nod slow, say nothing, then tread toward the dead animal and make a detour to the barn when Thelma's out of sight. I'm walking around the spine of the wreckage when I hear chanting coming from inside. Gloomy and droopy. My guts clench. The morning is brightening by the minute, but my insides are darkening and I can't go to where that chanting is. Not now, not ever.

Instead, I walk further along the spine where I left my yellows hanging over the washing tub. Find them curdled. I turn 'round, retrace my steps, grab a semi-filled pail of ash-lined milk leaning against a rake, then close by, a dead chicken, its feathers singed but otherwise whole. I plod back to the silo, my face puckered and my body throbbing and Bud on my tracks, slobbering.

What's wrong? Eve asks, watching me wheeze.

I've got a cold, I tell her, which given the general state of affairs sounds lame.

She cringes at the chicken dangling in my grip.

I don't eat meat, she says.

You don't eat meat.

No.

I place the pail beside her, then my own sorry self against the outside wall of the silo, stripping the feathers off the chicken. If it wasn't for this feasting flu, I guess I would be hungrier, which is a good thing, considering everything. When I'm done, I throw the carcass toward Bud. Then I wash my hands, enter the silo, and lie down next to Eve.

Daylight is streaming into the inky space, casting warm rays over our recovering bodies. My vision swims to the view I had from the water tower, of the electrical lines hanging like abandoned skipping ropes over a hemorrhaging sea, a sea no doubt rising after last night's offerings.

I wonder how we're gonna make it, I tell her. I've seen what's out there and it's not good.

You mean the barn? Eve asks.

That, too. It's a heap of metal and wood. Folks are either gone, or going loopy. Animals seem sane, though.

Eve sighs heavy.

Father's church folks were always loopy.

I shake my head.

What?

Nothing.

A pause hangs in the air.

Did Thelma make it?

I nod, cringing.

I need to go back to the barn, she says. See if anyone needs help. And to bury Samuel.

I gulp.

Just rest. They're taking care of all that. And I wouldn't go back just now. It's not ... safe.

Eve gazes at me for a moment, then drops her head to her wound.

Samuel told me how they found you in that tree hollow, I tell her.

I hesitate.

I'm sorry.

Another hesitation, this time stretched out.

I'd say we're fighting a losing battle, she says.

I look at her quizzical.

That's giving up before you've even tried.

She shrugs. Maybe it's called surrendering.

Surrendering's not giving up, I tell her. It's what comes beyond quitting.

You ever thought about not existing? she pushes. Like, how many days we got left here? Don't see no sense in waiting out the inevitable.

I eyeball her. She's just survived a snake bite and she's talking about quitting.

A few years back, I explain, my Pa was getting real aggressive. More so than usual. I ended up smashing a lamp over his head in self-defense. He was chiding me for skipping church. Church was all he knew. That and boxing and farming. Three things I was never interested in. Three things he hung his life on. It got too much—all that fear of being beaten up, or worse. So after that lamp incident, I took Ma's gun and hid it in case I ever needed to use it. Not for anyone else, but for a way out, you know? For me.

She stares at me. So?

I squint at her and almost leave it right there. She can stew in her own self-pity. I fan the fingers of my right hand and twist my forefinger into view. She gazes at the fault line running down its length.

Look, here. I've dealt with broken bones and sore muscles and swollen joints so bad, each time I broke or tore or swelled, my whole body started screaming something was wrong. Every bit of me was standing to attention, fighting to heal wherever pain was happening. It's amazing how the body fights.

Thing is though, bones and muscles and joints are housed under skin. Protected in their own casings. So the healing is quicker, the screaming muffled. Swaddled, you could say. But a deep cut? Now that's something else. That's a scream of a scream. That's a whole different fight.

I flex my forefinger closer to her gaze.

This happened when I was nine. Took one of Ma's kitchen knives and sliced an orange right through here. It gushed so much, it felt like I could have bled out on that cut. I remember just gazing at the gap, wondering if my body would shut off its own valve or let it bleed out if I just left it alone. Became dizzy just thinking about it.

Then my finger made that awful pulsing pump, like it does when your skin exposes your heartbeat? Felt as though my whole heart was leaking, so I panicked and grabbed an old hankie and stemmed the flow until I could find a big enough cloth. Even then, when the cloth went on, the pink soaked all the way through, rivulets of blood, then a sea of red right down my arm. I was dazzled by the sight, mesmerized. I got all this in me, I thought, all this life swimming 'round.

I realized right then and there that it was up to me to decide whether to keep bleeding or live. That day, I found I couldn't let myself go. I found a thicker cloth. Hasn't always been that way, you know. And up until now, right about now actually, I'm realizing that no one can stop tomorrow coming, but anyone can stop himself from coming into tomorrow.

So, I'm not saying nothing's more important than me, but my body is worth keeping alive because it tries keeping itself alive. Just like yours just did. Until it can't. Simple as that. Because of that.

Eve brushes her hair from her face and stares at me fierce.

Is that all you got?

I nod.

Then why did you say you didn't know if we were gonna make it?

I didn't say *if.* I said *how.* Me and Bud, we're still on our way to the coast. I wanna stick my toes in the sand.

This isn't a holiday, Jack, she snaps.

I bite back. No, it ain't. This is life, I snap back. If you want to bow out now, go ahead. But I'm not going down easy. It's called instinct—surviving like we have. Instinct and will.

A scowl scorches her face.

You haven't lived how I've lived, she balks. You weren't abandoned in a fucking tree!

Tears start colliding in her eyes. Fire ignites mine. I make a fist.

You have no idea how I've lived or how I goddamn haven't! And anyway, no one's going to bother if you kick the bucket, especially if you kick it yourself.

Is that so? she says, turning on me. Well, let me tell *you* something. I've been living on instinct all my life. I'm just sick of not living on much else. And speaking of not bothering about buckets, what are you doing hanging around trying to fill up mine?

My thoughts exactly.

She drops her gaze to my clenched hand and freezes. I'm combusting and about to strike until I realize

I'm about to strike and feel like shit for it. I lower my fist. Inhale deep. Exhale long.

Why'd you steal my gun? Huh? *Again?*

She blinks.

At that swamp, I press.

She blinks again, stutters.

I was trying to protect you.

Protect me.

Save you.

Save me.

Yes! Okay? From you getting bit. I was trying to save you.

I stare at her.

Then get busy saving yourself. 'Cuz no one else will.

I stomp right past, charge out the door and down the hill, leaving her staring out of the empty mouth of the silo.

Chapter Fifteen

Flick, flash, repeat, like a lighthouse coming 'round. I'm coughing madly, the tickle becoming an itch I can't scratch.

What are you doing? Eve asks quiet.

Saving my soul.

She swallows. Saving *our* souls, technically.

I frown. Only technically.

You really think that's gonna work?

Eve steps out the silo, watching me tilting her blade back and forth between the sun and the metal wall. I glance down and shut my eyes from the glare of the knife and the glare of the girl.

Samuel said emergency services would be on their way soon.

Eve raises her eyebrows.

Samuel said that?

Yeah, well, his gut said so. So.

The girl walks over and peers upwards. She's changed out of her robe same as I have. It's as much a relief to see her in normal clothes as it is for me to be wearing some.

It's not much to go on, but it's something, I say awkward.

It's a lot to go on.

It is?

Yeah.

Well, then.

My stomach flips while she keeps watching and I keep flicking.

Listen, she says tentative. I wasn't thinking clear before. About this surviving business. Can we just ... start over or something?

I offer a small smile. That's the idea.

This sparks another 'round of hacking, then a wallop of a sneeze. Eve grabs the bucket of water and hands it over while Bud makes his appearance, padding out of the bushes with feathers glued to his gums.

At least someone's belly's happy, I say, lifting the pail and drinking with cupped hands.

You didn't eat any? she asks.

No matches.

No backpack neither, I guess, she says, looking toward the barn.

No point even looking for it.

Eve dips into the silo and steps back out crushing something green and leafy in her hands. She hands the waxy wad over and the smell is stimulating and distinct. Fresh mint.

I raise my eyebrows.

Where did you get this?

Grows in lots of places, she says. You just need to know where to look.

She takes a pinch and starts rubbing the leaves over her teeth and tongue. I follow suit, then rinse.

Thanks.

No problem.

We sit in silence for a while.

Your father sounds like an asshole, she says suddenly.

I throw her a look, then sigh deep.

I gotta tell ya, for the first time I feel truly sorry for the old man. Sights set on a world that halted at the first hurdle. I kept an old photo of him, from the Navy. Never seen him look as proud as he was in that photo. All decked out in blue and white—the ship's helm right behind him, a huge wooden wreath—both of them scrubbed and primed for travel over seas wide and reaching.

145

I cup more water and splash it over my face and arms. Sigh again.

Pa once told me how he learned to swim. His own Pa threw him into the deep end. Just like that. Thought it was the best way to work things out. Thought his arms and legs would know what to do under threat. But Pa said arms and legs don't know what to do. They become jelly. No chance to warm up. That's why he started boxing me young. So I could have a fighting chance. So that I'd know what to do with my limbs.

Eve's gawking at me.

Your Pa almost drowned, she says straight.

Yep.

Did his Pa ever try that stunt again?

Nope.

So. I guess his Pa pulled him out.

Yep.

Why did he do it?

Pull him out?

No. Throw him in.

Like I said, he didn't know any better way to teach.

I start flicking the knife at the metal again, gazing at the heavens. The day's heating up, keeping some of the smoke trapped.

You know, Pa was always pushing me to join the Navy. I guess he wanted me to finish off what he started. Got as far as the Cadet Training vessel but jumped ship after he came down with a bad case of bullies. Senior Officers always give recruits a hard time but the pack was brutal that year. Pa just couldn't hack it. Took him an age to admit it to me. Well, he didn't tell me. His beer did. But there it is. He stuck with farming after that. Was something he always knew about anyway—how to farm. Though he never quite left the sea.

And your mother? she asks quiet.

What about her?

Was she around?

A smirk scratches my cheeks. That's a good way to put it. Ma was around all the time, but she was always looking the other way. And Pa did the opposite—he was always in my face. I could barely breathe either way, with either of 'em. I guess the only thing they had in common was that they were both searching for something.

She wipes dust off her pants and points toward the flattened trees.

There's some crabapple and walnut trees a bit lower down. I'm gonna collect as much fruit and nuts as I can, then head to the barn. See what can be shared out between us all.

I look at her. I told you it's not safe. I'd stay close to the silo until things start calming down some, alright?

How come?

Thelma. She's not thinking straight. If she knows you're alive, well, let's just say, she'll think the Devil is, too.

Her jaw drops. You serious?

Wish I wasn't.

She shakes her head, then glances at the barn still smoldering.

You know her well? The others? I ask her.

Sort of, she says solemn. Can we do questions another time?

I almost tell her she started it, but I offer a shrug instead.

She motions to the slope and starts walking.

Half an hour later, I'm heady from lack of food and an abundance of sun, so I enter the silo where Bud's dozing in a blissful curve against the wall. Lying flat on my back next to him, I let the slight breeze cool my limbs and the position de-clog my nose. Must be a minute or two, tops, before I shoot up again, shrieks and screams striking the silo's walls. Eve's shrieks, with Thelma's overtop and others layered between.

I yank on my boots and peer around the doorframe. Thelma's got a pitchfork in one fist, a large wooden cross in the other, and she's gaining on Eve who's yelling at me to grab my gun. I fumble in my jeans for it and Eve gets 'round the back of me, leaving a ten-foot stretch between us and Thelma and two men hobbling behind her—one old, the other older, eyes wide with wooden crosses aimed also.

I point my gun, and the men halt mid-hobble.

That a gun? Thelma shouts incredulous, halting now, too. She fiddles her eyeglasses and her cheeks flare crimson. That's a gun!

Lips pinched, she starts running at me with the pitchfork held horizontal.

I stumble into Eve, startled. Bud stumbles into me, and then the three of us stumble anywhere Thelma ain't.

A battle cry from the woman as we gain ground, swerving around pieces of plane, bolting northwards clear across the summit toward the horse field, its fence half up and providing no horses, but a level enough landing for something stirring yonder. Eve and I tilt our heads to the stirring. Faint wasps of wind growing wilder, then chopping the air in heavy clunks. A metal whale—flung from the floods, rising up and over the north side of Shackle, spinning its iron fins and sounding like hell's best attempt at heaven.

Chapter Sixteen

Bud's dancing his eyebrows and circling wild. I'm yelling and waving and Eve's weeping and waving and Thelma's just yelling. The men are hobbling the other way, crouching from the clamor. For a few seconds, the helicopter judders and figure-eights, then clocks us and flies straight. Bud ducks behind me. Eve covers her ears and together we're huddling under blasts of air while the ground goosebumps and the grass ruffles.

My lungs fill up with hope. The type Samuel went on about. The type with wings.

One of the pilots, a dark-skinned guy, gives us a thumbs up. The other pilot is winter-white compared and craning his head out the window, surveying the wreck of the barn instead of the wreck of us. There's a moment of indecision, the blue whale hovering, deciding where to beach. We're perched too close to the horse field. I tug Eve away from the fallen line of fence to give some space. Thelma's puffing and panting further back, in awe, shock, or terror, or maybe all three.

The helicopter lowers and its blades come to a complete stop. The pilots unlock their belts, unstrap their helmets, open their doors, and step down.

In the scramble and shuffle of the commotion, I forgot I'm still holding my gun. Fuck. I let it drop to the ground and place my foot over it casually while the men walk toward.

The dark-skinned guy's hair is sheared to a few inches and he's wearing a dark blue one-piece and black strapped boots, same as the paint work on the helicopter. He waves as they get nearer, an open smile. Winter-white's frowning, clothed in army gear, brick-red hair in tatty clumps. Not much older than us—mid-twenties, I figure. Hard to tell given their uniforms and stubble. We watch as the pilots stride closer and grow broader. Thick necks and tough handshake types. Boxer types.

When they're almost upon us, the open-smiled guy nods real official and extends his hand.

Benjamin.

I shake his hand. Eve introduces herself with a smile overspilling.

Benjamin turns to winter-white.

This is Reg. We're part of the county's rescue mission.

The other guy's frown's still etching.

Doesn't look pretty over there, Reg says. You the only ones who made it?

There's a few more, Eve says. The airplane hit the barn like a bomb.

No shit, Reg says, cocky. He keeps his gaze on Eve longer than a guy should. She throws me a glance and

I'm about to say something when Bud starts whining. He's right up close with his paw hung in the air. I bend down and cuddle it in my hand. Must have been damaged in his mad circling.

We'll check the barn before we head, Benjamin says. How many others are we talking about?

There's five of us left, Thelma responds from a distance.

She points at me and Eve. Excluding them.

She says *them* like we're sin on toast.

But we're not going anywhere, Thelma continues. We're waiting for someone else.

Benjamin rubs his chin.

You'll be waiting a long time, Ma'am. Rescue missions are getting thin on the ground.

Well, here's where I'm staying for now. Here's where I'm staying.

Thelma pleats her arms. Then she clasps the cross close to her chest, side-glancing Eve. The pitchfork is stabbing the ground beside her.

Reg whistles low and eyes Benjamin, then me and Eve.

You all aware of what's been going down?

Communication's been nil, I tell him. I tap my bare wrist. Been worried all this time how far the catastrophe's spread out. Is Sky Ship down or something?

Ship?

Station.

Reg cocks his head at me. How far do you think it's spread out?

I dunno, I say. Thought it was just our town at first. But, I dunno ... half the world?

He throws his head back. Sweet Jesus. It's bad, farm boy. I'll give you that. Thing is—

We don't know for certain, Benjamin cuts in.

The weather's hammering the southern coastline, running east to west, Reg continues. Ocean doesn't give a fuck who she washes over once she gets going. West coast is turning into east coast's weather big time—hurricanes are ripping straight past us. The Strait of Camerico is getting wider as we speak.

Benjamin grimaces. Sky Station's comms are scratchy, but basically—

The weather's gone ass about front, Reg interrupts. Like it did over half a century ago when Sky Station was invented to deal with this kind of crap ever happening again. And it better start dealing soon. If Mother Nature could talk, we'd know something, at least. Maybe we'd know where to land our drenched asses next.

Benjamin's jaw clenches but he otherwise stays mute. Reg spits on the ground, then scrapes his gaze over me.

Seems she's talking loud and clear to me, I say. Anyways, our options were starting to run pretty low around here. Glad you two showed up when you did.

Benjamin's dark eyes turn a darker shade of sad.

Options are running out everywhere. We've come across other survivors. Mostly along the coast. Mostly in ships. Morale is getting low. Gas is low, too.

He glances over my shoulder toward Thelma's flaming face, then to the wreckage beyond, then further still to the valleys and hills sunken and soaking.

To be honest, he continues, we're surprised to see anyone alive this far deep in the county. The further inland you go, the bigger the earthquakes, though that part of the disaster seems to be over. Storms are still rolling in. Our base is a hundred miles due east, on the Owls. On one of the campsites set for climbers. There's a decent medical hut, tents, a few provisions. "Go East" is the instruction so far from Sky Station. East, then up the coast. But in the interim, helicopters are flying to every raised pitching post and taking survivors to higher levels of elevation where the world's safer. Everyone will be living like goats for a while, but the water levels will likely back off in most places.

The Owls? I ask. You mean that mountain range near the coast?

More like *in* the coast. Anyhow, we're getting by, just. Resources are low. Relief efforts are finding it difficult to cover all areas.

How are you finding food?

It's finding us, Reg says. There's piles of creatures looking for grub themselves. Coming out of the woodwork day and night so it's easy pickings. Also, there's heaps of vegetation. Never knew so much shit grew up there.

So what's the plan? I ask.

Reg laughs. The plan?

He digs the toe of his boot in the soggy grass and a chunk flings to the side. He sets his blue eyes on Eve again. My fists clench and my foot presses down on my gun.

The plan is to live as long as we can so that others can keep living past us. Always been that way, always will be. There's no way the weather's gonna drown me before I get the chance to have a little fun.

He smirks at Eve.

Benjamin's lips clamp. Reg doesn't notice. He spits again on the ground, two inches from my feet. Jerry flashes in my vision. I go livid and clench my fists tighter.

Reg steps in front of me.

You got something to say, boy?

No, sir. Just mighty glad they sent their biggest and baddest to save us poor farmer folk.

Reg stomps right up to my face. Didn't see that coming.

Eve raises her hand like a stop sign. We've all been through a lot. As Jack said, we're glad you showed up. Let's just leave it at that. Okay?

She keeps her hand raised while me and Reg corner glare. He breaks first. I release my fists. Eve lowers her hand.

Thelma is booting it back to the barn, looking over her shoulder all the while like we're gonna pounce.

What's her problem? Reg asks.

Eve shrugs and points to the sky. Everyone has issues with management, she says. I guess it just depends which department you're in.

You mean Sky Station?

God Almighty.

Reg shrugs, smirking. Same thing, he says.

Benjamin wipes his hand over his jaw, turns toward the barn.

We should check out the situation over there and see if anyone else wants our help.

This time, I'm stop-signing.

Trust us, I tell him. You don't want to go there.

Silence, then submission.

Fine, he says. Is that all you've got on you? We've never been out this far at this late time of day. Caught sight of the smoke hovering over the hill, so we had to inspect, but we need to get back before dark. Our headlights are busted.

I look at Eve. Got everything? I ask her.

She mouths "knife?" and I pat my jeans, all discreet.

You? she asks.

Yeah.

I glance the ground, then back up at her, eyes widening.

We're good, she says, then pats her pockets, bulging with nuts and fruit.

Benjamin nods and motions to the helicopter. Reg is already turning on his heels and walking off.

You go on, I tell Eve. I need to check Bud's paw and see what's bothering him.

We exchange glances. She nods and starts walking. Benjamin and I watch her go.

She your girlfriend?

I smile despite myself. Don't know what she is.

He throws me a cheeky glance. I get it.

I look at him. Reg always a dick?

He chuckles. Being a dick's all relative at this stage of the game. These types of situations bring out the worst and best in people, plus everything in between. But yeah, Reg is a dick.

Benjamin rubs his jaw. Speaking of situations, he adds, how'd you escape the disaster in your part of the woods?

I stand up and wipe my hands on my jeans. Being stuck right in the thick of it, I guess. The ground split in front of me, at the edge of the forest. Somehow the rock I was lying on didn't budge. Was fast asleep when it all started.

He shakes his head.

Damn.

I shrug. Knew something big was coming, like I guess we all did. The droughts and all. But this big? Shit. Anyhow, I feel like I have a plan ahead of me. An out. You?

Pretty much the same thing.

I call Bud closer but he's not moving, kinda whining, so I take a few steps and lift his paw gentle.

Well, look at that, Benjamin says behind my back.

Fuck. Fuck. Fuck.

I release Bud's paw, stand up straight.

It's mine, I tell him flat.

The pilot has the gun in his palm. He gives me an eye-full before turning it over and rubbing the dirt off.

You sure about that? He says. He clicks the safety

catch while my mind's kicking myself at my clumsiness.

Glock 19. Nine inches. Loaded?

Two bullets, I mutter.

He checks the magazine. And you sure you're not one of them?

One of who?

He motions toward the ruined barn.

The crosses.

I exhale.

Never have been.

Well, God forgive me anyway, he says, and points the gun at his forehead.

My heart spasms. Then, just as quick, Benjamin laughs and lowers the weapon to his side and clicks the safety back on.

Not sure what you've done so far with this here weapon of yours, but I gotta say it ... that's what you need to do when things get nasty. Don't hesitate. Just do it. If I'm in your line of fire, shoot me first. You strike me as a good man—and good men make good choices—but those kinda choices gotta be made quick.

I shoot a glance at Reg with a wrench in his grip, fiddling with the engine. Eve's standing away from him, checking her pockets.

What are you getting at?

You know what I'm getting at, he says. Hell, you're the one who owns a gun.

He hands me my weapon sideways. I take it and shove it deep in my front pocket, shaking a little.

A cattle call. It's Reg, telling us to make a move on. We start walking, Bud limping at my side. I pick him up. We arrive to Reg tapping the glass of the cockpit window and Eve leaning against the passenger door. I release Bud and he shuffles over to Eve and wags at her. Reg is picking his nails now, bored as a schoolboy.

You made it then, he yawns.

Give it a rest, Benjamin snaps.

Reg shoots him a look, then opens the door of the helicopter and grabs his helmet off the seat.

We gotta get back pronto, *Captain.*

We'll be fine, Benjamin says tight. There's enough light left.

I'm not talking about the light. I'm talking about the gas. We got ourselves a leak.

Reg hands Benjamin the wrench. He treads to the engine, opens the hatch and twists the cap off, brow furrowing.

You good? I ask Eve, wiping my snotty nose.

She nods.

Benjamin seems decent enough. But that other guy—

Don't worry, I tell her. I've got your back.

I was going to say the same thing to you, she says, serious. Seems like he's got something against you.

And that would be you, I almost say.

Just stay calm, she says next. Least till we know what we're dealing with.

I look at her.

How'd you get so bold?

She shrugs. I was born bold.

She scours the barn, then me. You could have shot Thelma, you know. She's gone crazy.

I nod slow.

But you're not the killing kind, she says soft.

I shrug. Not sure I'm the fighting kind, either.

Her eyes start twinkling. Now, I wouldn't be so sure about that.

Benjamin steps up with a bottle of water.

The leak's small enough, he explains. Was able to tape it up, but I'll keep monitoring the situation. Trip will take forty minutes. When we arrive, you'll need your flu seen to and your dog's paw, too.

He glances at Eve's forearm, the double rainbow now an innocuous tattoo.

Damn. That a snake bite?

Yep.

He rubs his jaw. Damn.

Eve takes a swig from the bottle and hands it to me. I gulp the rest as she steps up and into the passenger seat. Then I hoist Bud up and buckle him in the middle seat, then belt myself. Benjamin flicks the switch and the blades kick into motion, but then they whirl down in a hurry.

What's going on? I shout above the din.

Benjamin points toward the barn.

Bodies are silhouetted against the ruins, like gray ghosts in the smoky haze. Ghosts with arms held flat against their bodies, staring head on. A line of defense, or offense.

Reg says something to Benjamin and the Captain nods. He flicks the button and the blades start rotating again.

Wait! Eve calls out, unbuckling and tapping Benjamin on the shoulder.

He keeps the blades rotating slow. Reg bucks against his seat, cursing. I unbuckle and follow Eve outside, standing attention while one of the ghosts steps forward.

She's petite, though growing larger by the second. One shoe missing, but walking steady.

When she gets close, I walk toward her. She holds out her palm and nods toward the helicopter.

He's come, Joan says.

I take her hand. Look her straight in the eye. You sure?

I told you Jesus was on his way, she says. And at this juncture, any which way will do.

Chapter Seventeen

The look on my dog's face as we start lifting.

This ain't the time to be scared of heights, I tell him, clenching my eyes and squeezing his fur and holding my breath as the blades whirl, the helicopter tilting and chattering loud as a whale's blowhole, and I'm glad I've got nothing in my belly to blow out. Next minute, Eve's hand clasps 'round mine and I open one eye to her pale skin glowing greener, too.

When the helicopter levels, Benjamin cranes his neck and gives us a thumbs up. I manage to give one back, forcing both eyes open which somehow calms the shakes. What's happening below is enough distraction, besides.

The roads are riverbeds, buildings are broken like bones, valleys have turned into lagoons. Everything once living or used by the living is floating aimless. Then, in the very far distance, the mountain range. I've seen photos of the Owls and their bordering harbor in local history books at school. My heart bumps against my ribs. I'm about to see a real harbor and a real sea, though from this distance I'm looking at a child's drawing—a thin, pencil-line horizon, lead colored.

Snowy Owl, white-capped and snuggled between Brown and Tawny, is standing narrowest and tallest. All three are perched on the edge of the coastline hungry for land. High tides would be an understatement. Can just make out what's left of the half-moon harbor straddling Snowy's shoreline—shaped like an old man's gum line with tiny teeth-boats tethered to the main dock. If a ship pulled up now, a sailor could almost step from the mountain straight onto the deck. I smile at that. Like I can see that happening—like I can see that happening to me. Suddenly, my insides feel better. Glancing at Eve, she's looking less reptilian, too. Bud's still frozen in shock, though at least he's staying put, and Joan, sitting opposite, hasn't stopped smiling since we took off. I watch her extend a hand to Eve. Eve takes it and squeezes.

Just when I'm relaxing some, Reg shouts something to Benjamin and points dead ahead. I peer through the gap between their helmets and see clouds miles away. Lots of them. Dark as ash. Benjamin motions back to where we came from. More head shaking and I can't hear much of anything until a waft of speech flies by my ear:

Freak storm.

Fuck's sake. My jaw tightens and a heavy eeriness settles into the small space. I'm waiting for Benjamin to turn and toss another thumbs up, but he's got both thumbs on the controls driving us down a different path. Banking sharp to the left. Turning away from the squall and heading toward the backside of the Owls. Reg barks at him again, gesturing wild. Then, out of nowhere and in one swift motion, Reg releases his seatbelt and—keeping one hand on his controls—whacks Benjamin on the side of his head with his fist. Then another thump, harder, jamming Benjamin's helmet up past his ear. His body rams against the door, then folds like a puppet on the floor. Eve yelps like a banshee and I snap my seatbelt off as Reg plonks down in his seat, his hands on the controls, levelling the helicopter's pitching.

What the hell are you doing? I yell at him. You're heading straight for the squall!

I reach past Joan toward the front and grip his shoulder, steadying more than threatening.

Keeping us the fuck alive, he yells back.

He tugs his shoulder from my grip.

I glance at Benjamin. No movement. Panic strips my insides. I think of my gun, but Reg's got his hands on a bigger weapon. I reach for Benjamin instead.

Leave him, Reg commands. I'm gonna skirt the worst, but this way we get a chance to land before it gets too dark to land at all.

I stare from one man to the other, to the mass of ash, yawning wide. Rain misting underneath.

Goddamnit, pilot, just get us through!

Nothing more to be said, nothing less to be done. I hobble to my seat, drop down into it, and yank the seatbelt across my shoulders like I'm making a cross.

Then I do make a cross for Bud and Eve and Joan. Just in case. Not wantin' any of them to go out under the joystick of some maverick prick.

I brace Bud as Reg dips the bow of the helicopter, dropping altitude. He banks right. Dips further and we dive near the pool of gray. The mist turns to rain and beats at the roof, wanting in. My belly is hollow and raining black. The rest of me, black and raining hollow.

Then everything's shaking thunder, rattle, dark. Every muscle's taut and I'm gripping and calling on whoever's up or below, asking to live till I can't ask no more. More thunder and rattle and raising up, down, then almost stopped. Then, after what seems like miles of rocking and rolling, the pool of clouds part to a pale pink and the metal whale starts blowing its usual thunder and swims level again. Nightmare turning doable dream. The sky turns back to sky and the Owls reappear through the jaws of a dusk still feeding on the day's dying light.

I sigh. Reg pumps his fist. Eve exhales and Bud's stiff as wood. Joan's not smiling anymore but at least she's not freaked. Her eyes are closed and her palms are touching. Everyone's settling down. I crane my neck to check on Benjamin still hibernating on the cockpit floor, unclasping my seatbelt as Eve shakes her head.

Let me, she mouths.

I watch as she gets up and leans close to Reg. A few words between them and she bends across Benjamin's seat, fingertips finding his neck pulse. She sends me a small thumbs up. Then she rips a bit of loose fabric from the bottom of her torn pants and pats at the blood still trickling from his ear.

I think I got a boo-boo, too, Reg taunts.

Eve ignores him, which calms me down an inch. Benjamin's chin is lifting and he's mouthing something and raising one arm like a tentacle looking for purchase. Tries pushing himself up with the other arm but gives up and collapses back to sitting. Eve holds him steady, buckling herself into the empty seat.

I lean back and look out the window, feeling less than useful but shivering with excitement because there it is. The sea. Spread out wide like it has all the time and right in the world. Lapping and quenching its own sweet self. The sight would be overwhelming enough on level ground let alone from such dizzying heights, and seeing it now—bluer than blue, deeper than deep, far bluer and deeper than the sky above and earth below—in this moment, it doesn't matter if the world's going or already gone because for the first time ever, I'm headed somewhere that ain't home.

I peel my eyes from the water to the mountains and notice shutters of light flicking the peaks and more light haloing the mountain top, making the snow glisten like angels playing. Looks like we're heading straight for Snowy since we're passing stumpy Brown on the port side, the harbor changing size from half-moon to quarter. A sprinkling of what looks to be fireflies start sparking along the lower rim of Snowy's face. The closer we get, and the fireflies morph into a path of tea-lights lit in paper bags—a path that leads to a makeshift landing pad with a white cross painted in the middle. A few hands are waving. The helicopter hovers closer and drops, and the air whirls around a man and woman who are running closer to the pad. The woman's hair is standing on electric-shock-end and her nurse's apron is almost blowing off. Reg is grunting loud, grounding the aircraft like he's slapping down a toy.

Cursing and gripping the handle above my seat, I grip Bud's furry neck as we fully land. The landing pad is a square piece of sandy soil with boulders shouldering. The man's a splitting image of Reg, only older, with short-cropped white hair instead of russet, and leathery skin and hunched shoulders. The woman is younger, brown skin, dark curls pulled in a ponytail, wearing white like a wedding. She hangs back for a second, waiting for the blades to settle down. When the man gets close, he stops and squints at the cockpit, rubbing his long stubble. I rub my own scratch of sand. Before anyone can say anything, Reg whips his helmet off, opens the door, and exits.

Wonder what version he's gonna give, I mutter to Eve. She scowls.

Benjamin's coming to life. While Eve steadies him, he releases his helmet strap with shaky fingers. Red is blooming along his jawline. Balancing on the door frame, he opens the window and spits out a mound of pink gob, then fires his eyes toward Reg. Clouds of smoke billow from his nostrils in the chilled mountain air. If he could charge, he would.

You got knocked out bad, I tell him. Think that's the worst of it, though. Still, the bastard needs some reckoning with.

Benjamin glowers. Keeps his voice low.

Leave it be. His time will come.

He spits another round out the window while I gawk at him. Have to bite my tongue from arguing the matter.

I motion toward the two men standing profile.

That his Pa?

Benjamin nods, touching the wound by his ear. He winces as fresh blood spills.

Stay out of his way, too.

The woman in the white pants and coat strides forth with a first aid kit in her grip. She steps up and enters the cockpit, eyes flitting at Joan and Eve before holding her gaze on me. She brushes her fingers through her dark fringe.

I'm Sierra, she says. Head Nurse. Who needs attention first?

I nod toward Benjamin, then at Bud still strapped in his seat behind her line of vision. The nurse cocks her head and grins at my dog, then places the kit on the co-pilot's seat and opens the lid. She pulls out scissors and a roll of bandage.

The medical hut is closest to the landing pad, she says. We'll get you over there first. She steps toward Benjamin and starts wrapping the bandage snug around his head, then mops up the blood on the seat.

What happened here?

Short story, Sierra, he says. Just focus on getting these guys comfortable.

You know the protocol, Ben. Everyone needs to check in.

Sierra makes to say something else, but sighs instead and closes the kit. She looks out of the cockpit window at the two men talking in hushed tones. My muscles tighten.

I just overheard Reg telling Saul where he found you all, she says. Thought there'd be no one left to find. Was worried you wouldn't make it back at all, Ben—I saw that storm brewing over the ocean. Like we haven't had enough thrown at us. She turns to us. Anyways, welcome to the Owls. We operate like a border control so you'll all be scanned. We're pretty much it in terms of population count in this county, so we have to know who's going in and out.

I expect her to say more but she starts collecting her kit.

You've got enough power to do scans? I ask her.

I don't mean that type of scanned, she says. I mean old fashioned body checks.

Eve and I exchange glances. My hand travels over my front pocket.

Movement outside of the helicopter. Reg and the older man are approaching. At the same time, Bud starts wriggling, wanting out. I hobble toward him, unbuckle and hook him under my right arm while the older man enters the cockpit. Reg lags behind, his face a mixture of sheep and wolf.

Griffith. Saul.

The man stretches his hand but it's not matching the one I can shake with so I just nod.

Jack. Scott.

Scott, welcome.

No, that's my last name.

He raises an eyebrow, then turns to Eve.

Eve, she says, reaching a hand.

He offers a wide grin, then turns to Benjamin, frown taking over.

Reg filled me in on what happened out there. Said you were putting everyone in more danger than was necessary. Said part of the storm was a lot flimsier than you made it out to be and he was able to get through the heart of it in a flash. That so?

Benjamin exhales. You'll have to ask them. I was otherwise occupied.

Saul eyeballs him, then turns to me. So?

Yep, I say sharp, glaring at Reg. All show and no substance.

A pause rings the air.

Then we're good, Saul says. There won't be any more rescue missions, anyhow. Too little fuel, too little time. We need to stay put and prepare for what's coming.

He tips his head toward me, Eve, and Joan.

Consider yourselves fortunate. You're the last survivors we'll find.

Joan wipes her brow and stands up wobbly. I steady her while Saul announces that night's drawing in soon and we have to make a move. Reg exits first, then Benjamin with Sierra walking alongside, balancing him all the while, followed by Eve, then Joan. I tag along with Bud tucked in my arms, Saul taking up the rear. After five or six steps, we all halt. A howling in the far distance, toward the top of the mountain. Faint but forceful.

Wolves, Saul says to my back. Been hovering for days.

Eve tilts her head to the peak. A shiver shoots up my ribs.

Reg starts walking again, cautious. We follow on, listening to the howling ebb and flow then finally go, my attention turning to the path that's narrowing abrupt, the cliff edge looking way too close for comfort. I keep my eyes pinned on Joan's back. When we get almost clear of the boulders leaning against the rock face, I look over my shoulder and tell Saul I have to relieve myself.

He grimaces.

We're on a roll here, boy, he says. Can't it wait?

I make a face. Been holding it in all flight.

Another grimace and he nods to the largest boulder and I lever myself around the back of it. I lower Bud and squat out of sight, taking my time, fishing out the gun and knife and stuffing them in a deep enough slit in the rock with a noisy round of coughing. By the time I'm done, Bud's back in line, next to Eve.

All good? she says, patting him tender.

Yeah, I tell her. All good.

Saul motions us to continue. I pick up Bud and follow Joan, Saul treading close behind.

A few minutes later and I'm smelling pine needles and wood smoke and cigarettes and hearing the faintest traces of female voices and a cluttering of pots. A dozen more steps and the narrow ledge widens to a flat sheet of grassy land with hiking paths like veins leading up the mountain side.

As generic a base camp as I've ever seen and I may as well be looking at a crowd of Girl Scouts sitting 'round a fire roasting marshmallows and singing "Kumbaya." There's a handful of men sprinkled, a girl with bright orange hair huddled close to an older woman, but mostly women, around thirty in number, sitting on tarps and flattened backpacks. We walk closer and they stare at us, weary and a few wary. Not smiling, and definitely not singing.

Hikers? I ask, uneasy.

Saul nods.

A few guides too, plus Sierra to deal with any injuries. You could say she's been kept busy, treating minds as well as bodies.

Eve stops walking and I almost bump into her. She turns 'round and stares at Saul with turquoise eyes dimming.

That's it? she asks. No one else managed to get up here?

A few locals climbed up, he says, shrugging. And those that didn't climb, crawled.

How did you make it up? I ask him.

He clears his throat. Reg and I flew in with Benjamin.

How many others have you rescued by helicopter since then?

Three. Plus you two.

I shake my head. Those are small numbers.

That's reality. Anyways, a bigger rescue's on its way. Could be in a day or two, but I'm guessing sooner, as this calamity seems to be wrapping up and the wind's blowing in the right direction for us to keep moving east.

There's movement in the crowd. It's the girl, leaning away from the older woman and beelining to Saul. Up close, her face is a splash of freckles.

Sir? she says, bouncing on her toes. Is the cruise ship coming soon?

He scratches his head. Yes.

How soon?

Don't know.

The girl wrings her hands.

I think another storm's coming.

Could be.

It is, she says. My skin's getting itchy again. Bobby's up the mountain, keeping watch.

Saul rolls his eyes. Could be.

So, how soon—

Christ Almighty, he groans, tapping his wristpod. Like I keep telling everyone, communication's still patchy. Soon as I know, you'll all know.

He waves her away. She dips her chin, timid, then

tosses me, Eve, and Joan a glance before walking back to the campfire. Joan taps Eve on the shoulder.

Let's go and introduce ourselves to the group, Joan says.

Not till you pass the body checks, Saul instructs, pointing to the medical hut yonder. They nod, and start walking. Bud squirms out of my arms, wobbling after them.

I follow Saul's gaze toward the sea. The view's partly obstructed by a thick curve of rock, but there's a gap showing white-capped waves.

Where's the cruise ship gonna take folks? I ask.

East coast. The storms keep traveling west so we've likely had the worst of it. There are bigger refugee camps there, plus better means to get the displaced back to where they came from when this all clears up.

The man looks toward the sky. Sighs heavy.

We had all the technology to pin something up in space, he says, but some beastly weather comes along again, and just like that, our Sky Station, with all its shiny bright energy, turns into a rusty old juke box. Beginning to wonder just what the Station's up to, he adds, then sighs again and starts walking away. I stare after him.

What do you mean—what the Station's up to?

Saul freezes in his tracks, turns 'round slow, rubs his jaw.

It's classified, understood?

He draws the words out and I swallow hard, almost choking on my spit. A memory's just pushed through, something Pa told me ages ago.

You alright, boy?

I nod through my coughing fit, mind spinning.

You sure about that? he says sour.

I'm aching to ask more, but his glare alone makes me step back and stay mute.

This little discussion we've just had? he says. This stays between you and me, or else you won't be staying anywhere. Understood?

I nod twice.

Wait and sit still is all you gotta do. East coast is our best shot. Like I said, there's enough refugee camps to hold fort until we can all go home.

Saul turns on his heels and starts walking away again.

I can't help it, my mind spins out another question before I have a chance to rein it in.

What if people don't want to go back to their homes?

He scoffs over his shoulder. You can try going wherever the hell you want to, but people don't much like outsiders in a crisis. We've just got to get out of this mess.

We will, I say.

He slows his pace.

That so?

We have to, I tell him. Else what's the point of escaping home in the first place?

Chapter Eighteen

Saul taps his foot.

This way, he says, steering me toward the tent with a white cross pinned on the flap. Night's drawing in quick, so we'll all eat after Sierra sees to you next. You like goat?

I run my tongue over my bottom lip. Right about now, I like anything, I reply.

Another forty steps and we arrive at the medical hut. Sharp light from an oil lantern hits my eyelids, making me sneeze in Saul's face. He recoils.

The majority of us have just gotten over a cold, he barks. Best you stay out of everyone's way till you recover. He walks away while I mumble an apology.

When I enter the tent, Sierra walks over with a Kleenex. Offers an empathic smile. Behind her, a cotton screen is pulled between two cots and I see Benjamin's shadow. He's lying on his back, unmoving. Bud's positioned himself in the nearest corner, licking his paw. Joan's standing by one of the windows. Eve's gone.

Your friend's making her way to the campfire, Sierra

says, clocking my worried expression. She showed me the snake bite, too. Looks okay. Lucky girl.

I nod in relief while the nurse motions to Joan.

I'll check your clothes first.

Joan walks forwards, arms raising up, fingers lifting her gold cross necklace for all to see. The nurse runs her hands over Joan's ragged dress and tights, then asks for the lone shoe. Joan bends down, slips it off, hands it over.

That feels better, she says, grinning.

Sierra smiles back. You're welcome at the campfire too, she says. We'll all join shortly.

Joan nods and exits the tent. As she does, a shriek punctures the air.

I sprint past Saul and Sierra. Folks are spilling out of their tents, rushing, a few tripping over jars filled with lit tealights. They start congealing around a boy emerging from the far path, bloody and mangled and staggering toward. Closing in on the boy with a torch limp in her hand, the freckled young girl is hysterical, still shrieking, yelling at an older woman who breaks free and rushes across the campsite. The woman's a few feet away when the boy collapses to the ground, thudding hard, neck spilling liquid and legs stretching limp like the stuffing's been taken out. The woman lunges and lifts the boy's shoulders, tears raining down her chin and onto his cheeks, blending with his blood. The girl is a lump of thundering gasps beside them.

Help! she cries to the crowd.

Saul gets to them first.

He shouts loud. Sierra! Supplies!

The nurse is right behind him, near on colliding into his shins. She pushes him out of the way and thrusts her fingers to the boy's neck. Blood pumps even more. After a few useless moments, Sierra releases her fingers, wipes her forehead, anguish and red streaks smeared across her face. Her hands drop to her knees, then one arm lifts and wraps around the woman's heaving shoulders.

Cila. He's gone. Bobby's gone, Cila.

The woman starts wailing and Sierra starts rocking her, looking toward Saul, who's looking toward a woman with a cot sheet wrapped around her arms. Saul steps over and takes the sheet to Sierra. The nurse nods, then says hush to the mother,

There's nothing we can do now. He was trying to do good. You know that.

Saul fans the sheet over the boy's body. Cila rips it back off.

Don't! she bawls.

Saul doesn't protest. Instead, he lays the sheet next to her and treads straight past the crowd, chin lowered, fists in balls.

Folks begin stepping away, a tide turning and heading in different directions, forming small knots of discussion. I overhear snippets from the nearest knot: West side. Above the treeline. Son's favorite lookout spot.

I spot Eve alone, hovering afar, hand covering her

mouth and eyelids shut tight. Then she opens her eyelids and slumps away. As I make my way toward her, something hard taps my shoulder and my muscles almost spring out of my body. It's Reg. Snarling.

You and your mangy dog should be back in that tent, farm boy. Far enough away to keep from infecting everybody. In fact, I think we should cage your snooping animal. Keep him from sniffing 'round our food stock.

I'm about to fire something back when Joan walks over, pointing her finger at Reg.

Quiet, you, she says strong.

He smirks and motions to the wailing mother. You should be telling that to her. Who knows how many people have died around her, and she's acting like it's happening for the first time.

The biggest smirk I've ever seen on a human being, and the biggest fist I've ever seen on me, and I punch that son of a bitch square in the face. Just like that. Knuckles to nose. And down he goes. Just like that. Next, Joan's at my side, guiding me back to the medical tent with the crowd staring on—a crowd stunned, and silent.

Chapter Nineteen

Sierra dips a second cloth in a bucket of water and wipes the rest of death off her arms and neck. She steps inside the medical hut, me tagging along under her instruction.

Your turn, she says somber.

Takes me a second to register what she's talking about, but then she points to my shirt, mouths "scan," and I raise my arms. The nurse travels her fingers down my chest to my jeans. I blush a touch, then take my boots off and put them back on in a hurry, embarrassed by the stench. Sierra nods the all-clear.

The girl doing okay? I ask her.

Sierra sighs.

She's with her mother.

Footsteps thunder toward the tent. The nurse and I exchange glances. A whip of the flap and Saul barges in, stomps right up, wraps his fingers 'round my throat.

You lay a finger on my son again, or do anything else just as stupid, and I'll throw you clear off this mountain, got me?

He's about a foot taller and two times wider than me and I can feel the bruises already marking my skin.

Sierra steps up.

You didn't see what happened. Reg was provoking him.

Saul ignores her. Grips tighter.

You got me?

I try nodding.

Good.

He releases his fingers and glances at Benjamin. Cila lets out another wail outside.

I'm going to eat, he announces. That's about all we can do for the time being. Then I'm going to check the signal. At this rate, by the time Sky Station tells us the ship's arrival time, it'll be right in front of us, docking.

Don't mind him, she says in his wake. Stress does that to people.

Does what? I rasp.

Turn them into the type of person they've always been, underneath.

The nurse sighs and walks over to Bud.

So. What happened to this little guy's paw?

Rubbing my neck, I ease my body onto the cot.

He went mad when the helicopter arrived. Think he stubbed it or something. He's not making much noise about it, but I know he's hurting.

She crouches next to him as I get comfortable on the mattress. Feels like luxury. Makes me think of who's lying on the other bed.

How you doing over there? Benjamin?

He's sedated, Sierra says. Been under a lot of strain.
I keep mum.

Your dog's a cutie, she continues. What breed?

Cross between a mutt and a mutt.

She laughs, then gives him another pat before inspecting his paw.

I'm no vet, she says after a minute, but he's better off than he looks. Some swelling is all.

She cuts a strip of bandage and wraps his paw, then slides a bowl of water under his muzzle. Bud gives her a small lick, sniffs the bandage, then drinks like a funnel. She grins and touches the gray head of the stethoscope hanging around her neck while she walks over. When she plants the cold coin on my chest, asking me to inhale deep, a coughing fit erupts.

Hold on, she says. I think we've got something for that cough.

She walks away and a vision comes swooping of Ma holding a spoon to my mouth years ago. A rare moment of Ma paying much attention. Medicine for mumps. Vile tasting and scarlet red. Was barely able to hear what she was saying due to clogged ears and a raging fever making everything dim and dopey, so she said it twice.

Illnesses like these make you stronger, son. The illness, and the medicine. And you need to be strong because you're meant for a healthier life than this. A blooming life. You hear me? A blooming life.

A pat on my forearm breaks the vision.

Sorry, Sierra says. We're all out of medicine.

It's okay, I tell her, tasting the scarlet anyway.

She wipes her brow. Smiles.

We'll all be out of here soon enough, with any luck, she says.

I consider her.

Excuse me for saying, I start, but you seem pretty upbeat compared to the rest of the group, especially taking into account what's just happened.

Oh, I'm used to living it rough.

That so?

Yep. Spent half my life in the mountains, and half of that working as a nurse for hiking and skiing competitions. Seen lots of injuries. Fatalities, too. My dad used to take me camping all the time as well. Makes your skin tough. Literally.

The nurse pauses. Rubs her brow.

Don't get me wrong, though. There was panic at first. Plenty of it. That wave was petrifying. I was waiting here for the group to finish their hike and they had almost arrived when the ocean changed. From our elevation, it looked like a big soup bowl spilling over. So wide reaching. Couldn't see the beginning or end of it. The sight was breathtaking. The sound when it broke against the mountain, though? That wasn't a sea sound. More like the earth was roaring. A giant mumbling crunch. Terrifying.

She continues after a pause. For a second, I wasn't even scared—I was just totally in awe of it. Of what our Earth could do. But then all hell broke loose. That one wave kept rising and rising, crushing most of the harbor, the trees. Everything. The way that hiking group scurried like a bunch of mice ... seemed like the water was coming right up to our ankles, that's how it quickly it rose. Days back, it was much higher than it is now. I guess that's a good sign. The earth's starting to sponge herself up. Mother Nature is a wondrous thing.

Bullshit.

We snap our heads to Reg bulldozing the entrance, purple patches lapping his eyelid. Bud wobbles past him out the door, cocking a leg by the nearest bush. Reg ignores us both and strides toward Sierra, making to smack her on the butt.

Mother Nature's a raging, hormonal bitch, that's what.

Sierra springs away just in time.

Geez, Reg. Nothing keeps you down, does it?

He whistles some half-baked tune, warbling and rocking on his heels and he's tipsy. Can smell it on his breath. Sour beer.

Dinner's ready, he whispers at her neck. I'd be glad for a bit of company.

She offers a smile before pulling away.

Not tonight, big boy. I'm on duty.

That so? Reg says, turning and staring at me cold and sharp.

His scowl turns into a sloppy grin while he stumbles across to Benjamin.

Looks to me like things are all wrapped up here.

Reg whacks Benjamin's leg and he jerks awake. I spring up. The guy isn't drunk. He's deranged.

Leave him alone, I tell him.

Reg stomps over, lips tight, fists tighter.

You want to tell me that again, farm boy?

Sierra steps over.

Stop it, she says.

She throws me a look and steps closer to Reg.

Come on, let's go.

She's pulling at his shirt but he's still thinking about it.

Tell me, farm boy. What kind of work you get up to on that farm of yours? Milking cows? Plucking weeds?

I stare at him, words catching.

Uh huh, he says, nodding. Anything else?

I boxed.

His lips twitch. That so? A boxer.

No. Just boxed.

He squints, leans a little away. Uh huh.

Come on, Reg. Let it go.

You and me? He leans on Sierra, eyeballs me, straightens up. We got to work this thing out. We gotta work this here thing out.

He punches the last words and swerves toward, but Sierra pulls him back and steers him to the flap.

Hey. You okay? I ask after her.

She stops short, glances over her shoulder, walks on.

Hey!

I follow her out of the tent. Reg's stumbling ahead of her now, swaying, holding a hip flask and tipping it to his lips. I grab Sierra's elbow and she spins around.

I'm trying to help you, she says.

You don't have to do this, I tell her. I can stand up for myself.

She places her hand on my chest and looks me straight in the eye. Like I said, Jack, I'm used to living rough.

I hold her gaze for a moment, then watch as she turns on her heels and catches up to Reg. She reaches for his waist and he swings a heavy arm around her shoulders. They join the campfire, where I spot Eve standing in line with an empty plate waiting to be served. Willing myself to calm down, I re-enter the tent and pull the curtain across to find Benjamin on his back, mumbling something. On the bedside table, there's a box of aspirin and a bottle of valium and another bottle of another something. He's awake, though his eyes are fluttering. I walk over and stand next to the cot. After a few minutes of listening to garble, the flap opens and Eve walks in with Bud following, holding the plate piled with meat plus the rest of her nuts and fruit.

Hey there.

She steps toward and hands me the meal, then goes to Bud, pulling a fatty bit of bone from her pocket. His tail thumps the ground. I sit on the cot and start digging in at the same time as my dog. Now that I've started chewing something, I'm ravenous. Eve watches us gorge.

Tell me you've eaten, I ask her.

She shrugs.

Berries, mostly. Plus a can of rice and peas. There's stores left. The woman I was sitting next to told me there's a permanent bunker dug in the ground for emergencies.

Guess this is one of those emergencies.

Eve lowers her voice. Where did you put the knife and gun?

A cavernous yawn from Benjamin and Eve jolts. I hold a finger up.

He's sedated, I whisper.

She raises her eyebrows and walks toward him, looming over his chest. He sputters syllables. Then, out of nowhere, his fingers reach out and clamp her forearm. Eve flinches, then she slants closer, listening to his mumbling.

You're in the medical tent along with me and Jack, she says gentle. We're not going anywhere. It's heading to nighttime, anyway. Just rest.

Benjamin's head sinks back into the pillow.

No time, he mutters.

Benjamin?

She rubs his shoulder but his eyes are closing and his muscles are slackening and his breath is going back under.

I gobble the last bites and stand next to Eve.

Something ain't right, I tell her. Saul. Benjamin. Reg. He came in here just now. Drunk. Threatening. Spouting stuff. I know I hit him and all, but—

You did?

Yeah.

I look for a reaction but she stays neutral. I also don't like the way he looks at you, I say.

Eve's white cheeks go pink. I saw him just now with Sierra, she says. They look ... close. Eve swallows. Are they?

You asking if they're a couple? I watch her cheeks go pinker. Yeah, I guess they are. How come?

How come what?

How come you asking?

I—I just wanna know. He makes me uncomfortable, so it's good he's with someone. With Sierra, she adds, awkward. I nod, shrug poker.

Eve swallows again. A man sitting next to me at the campfire said everyone's starting to unravel, acting stranger every day, especially Saul.

I try sounding neutral.

187

Saul told me the weather's moving on and resources are in place. So.

You mean the cruise ship that's coming?

I inhale sharp. Nod.

If there's still a world out there, I tell her, then there's still a way outta this one.

Chapter Twenty

The night goes by in a flash. No nightmares. No dreams, even. Which is strange. Guess my wound-up mind needed some serious winding down.

I pull the woolen blanket off my warm body and sit upright on the cot. Benjamin and Bud are both snoring sporadic. Eve's peering out the tent's mesh window, rubbing her eyes.

Hey, I whisper. What's happening?

She turns her head. Whispers back.

Breakfast.

Yawning, I stretch my limbs and join her. Smoke's curling upwards from the main firepit. A large, muscly woman is stoking the coals. Joan and another woman are standing beside her, helping the proceedings. Reg is spouting something to another young guy, a steaming cup of something in his palms.

If only we were just camping, Eve says sad.

Yep. And if only we weren't dealing with the same kind of pricks I've dealt with my whole life.

What Eve whispers next is so quiet, I can barely hear.

Joan saw Reg almost kick Bud yesterday, when Sierra was busy with your body check. She said Bud was padding around the campfire before turning back to this tent when Reg near on tripped over him.

My face flares red.

Eve shakes her head. I shouldn't have told you.

Oh, you should have, alright.

No, she responds. Things are tense enough as they are. We just need to stay low. Wait for rescue.

I rub my jaw, hesitate, then address her square on.

There's something you should know, Eve. Something Saul said just after you and Joan started walking to the medical tent.

Her expression darkens.

Go on.

Sky Station. What's your understanding?

The girl frowns.

Understanding of what?

Of why it's hanging up there.

Weather vane, plus electricity monitor and back-up source? She scans my expression. I stay poker.

Parish never had much to do with it, she continues. Well, it never had much to do with us. We got on fine without its help. Father said we had God to provide, guide, and protect us. So.

I raise an eyebrow.

What?

Nothing.

What? she demands.

The louder pitch wakes up Bud. He rises, stretches, and wags himself over, gait looking much stronger.

I squint my eyes at her.

You believe in all that protecting and guiding. It's more a statement than a question.

She sets her jaw.

Go on, Jack.

I shift on my feet.

It's just ... you'd think Sky Station would be giving folks more information on what's happening. I get why radio waves wouldn't reach folks inland what with all the mayhem, but surely this mountain's got more reception. Why didn't Sky Station warn us, or at least tell us more when the shit hit? *Before* it hit? How come there's still been no information other than telling everyone to go east?

Eve's eyes dance distress.

What did Saul tell you?

He used the word classified. He's not fully in the loop, though.

I pause.

There's more.

I back us away from the window and steer her to the furthest corner, pointing at Benjamin's curtain. He doesn't seem to be stirring, but his snoring's stopped.

I tilt my head close to hers.

It's just ... it made me think of something Pa told me, ages ago. When he was drunk, obviously. He said that during his stint on the sea, he overheard the captain talking to some officials about how Sky Station didn't bother with citizens living too far afield, meaning isolated farm folks like us. Weather and electricity updates, sure, but to those living in more civilized areas? Information was provided regularly, on security and threats and such. I'd sheer forgot he'd told me that until Saul started talkin'.

Eve's jaw drops.

What else did your Pa say?

Nothing. He never found out more, and I wasn't gonna push him. Was too young to take much notice of shit like that, anyway. In any case, that's how he termed Sky Station "Ship in the Sky." Said it was as distant and inaccessible as a vessel lost at sea.

So what you're saying is—

I scratch my head, thinking.

I don't know. But it seems like comms being "down" might not be true for everyone. Like maybe they're keepin' stuff from us on purpose. *Just* us.

Fuck, Jack.

I know. Listen. What you said just now, about staying low? That's what we're gonna do. We gotta keep low and keep watch for anything—

Bud barks. Loud.

Quit it, I snap in a hush. But he barks again. Next second, the tent shivers from a bustle of movement. He dashes to the front flap, panting madly.

Eve throws me a worried glance and darts toward him. I follow, and we exit in a rush toward a group of people gathered. The freckled girl's standing and pointing toward the horizon.

I knew it! she blurts.

The girl sprints to the path linking campsite to

landing pad, the crowd on her heels with Eve and I flanking, our jaws dropping at the sight of a massive blanket swirling amongst the clouds. For a moment I'm hoping it's the cruise liner, making a grand entrance.

No such luck.

A whole host of slate-gray tornadoes are spinning down from the sky and hitting the water, dozens of them, growing in rage and speed and coming straight for the mountain.

Goddamnit.

Saul's baritone behind me. He pushes past layers of people and peers at the waterspouts, racing closer every second.

Everyone in the bunker! He commands. Where's Reg? Someone get Reg. Get everyone.

A mess of legs and scrambling back and forth between tents and bunker, Eve, Bud, and I rushing back to the medical tent. The pilot's sitting upright on the cot, rubbing his eyes.

What's happening? he asks.

We gotta go, I say, breaking into a cold sweat. There's another superstorm, or whatever the hell, heading our way.

Benjamin groans and stands up wobbly. Looks like he's about to faint. I hitch his arm over my shoulder. The gale's picking up big time, the air stirring thicker.

Hurry! Eve snaps.

No shit.

You wait here with Bud, I instruct, grabbing the

stethoscope from the bedside table. Tie a collar out of this. I'll get Benjamin across first.

She nods, grabbing Bud by the scruff of the neck. I brush past, guiding the pilot out of the flap, treading toward the bustle of people scurrying 'round and crowding the bunker's entrance, open to the elements. The space is small and filled with boxes. I keep asking for someone to take his weight, but no one's listening. People are stacking boxes, making space, crushing themselves in. Panicked, I lean him against the bunker's outer wall.

I'll be right back.

I got it from here, Benjamin says, though he's muddling his words and saying it to the wall.

Running back, the rusty flames of dusk now snuffed out, the wind rushing against my chest, I find Eve holding Bud, leashed, his eyes wide and looking ready to bolt.

Go! I shout at Eve, taking the collar and pulling Bud to my heels. She opens the flap, makes a sprint for it. Next moment, me and my dog are doing the same.

The wind's now a whirlin' dervish, flicking cold and damp and threatening. I get to the packed bunker, crouching next to Eve. The door's shut. Its iron gate clamped. I try opening it. Locked.

Eve and I stare at each other. I bury Bud in my arms. Benjamin's got his head and hands against the wall, bracing himself. He shifts his weight and clocks me and if anything, the gale is snapping him out of his stupor. He thumps one hand against the bunker, clutches his bandaged head with the other.

I'm looking for exits, entries, a miracle. Eve's banging on the door, but it's a mute needle in a thunder-roll haystack. I motion to the back of the stone shelter, a slight ledge providing an ounce of coverage. Eve tugs at my shirt and points to the nearest path up the mountain.

You kidding me?

We'll climb above the storm!

I motion to Benjamin. No, we won't.

Facing the squall, I spot a gap along the thick curve of rock, the same gap that exposed those winking waves yesterday. From this angle, I can see the boulders we passed on our way to the campsite.

I grip Benjamin's shoulder.

Can you walk?

He bobs his head.

Then follow me.

Holding Bud close, I yell at Eve to follow us. She's gawking at me, disbelieving.

No time to explain, only to act. Sand swirling, stones sling-shotting, I push into the oncoming tempest and duck behind the medical tent, the fabric roof ballooning, pegs pulling. Benjamin and Eve catch up and we shuffle our way past the rock toward the gap. The current of wind tides us through and we brace ourselves on the path. It's dark and treacherous. The gale wallops our faces as we edge across. I point to the boulders.

Benjamin's shouting something. I glance back. Eve's

semi-concealed behind a stubby stone. Benjamin's balancing precarious on a thin strip of ground on the other side of her.

Thinking quick, I turn 'round and spot the fat boulder that's hiding the gun and knife, perched five feet yonder. I skirt along and twist into the constricted space, then stuff Bud in. He leans against the rock face like a magnet to iron. Twisting back out, I watch as Eve leans out a little, shouting something to Benjamin. He grips her stretched arm and edges past but then falters, pulling Eve out of the socket and she's swaying and slipping and a scream the size of space when she almost falls off the cliff edge.

Holy Jesus Fuck. I'm yelling and bracing against the rock just feet from her as she clings to the rock face, the wind and wet pinning her to it.

Eve!

She turns her head and I reach out, motioning. Hair unknotted and flapping wild, she starts inching her way. A foot between us now. I reach for her arm and she's reaching too, but then a simultaneous sting of spray and whip of wind sucks her away and she flaps the other way, back slamming into a wall of rock.

Ticks of time pass. Almost slipping over the goddamn edge myself, I'm inching and reaching and she's staring at me, eyes flashing fear and fight, calm and surrender, and it takes all my might to keep looking at those eyes and keep holding on and I've got her but I don't know if she's got me.

Come on.

The wind's still pinning her and I've got her and I'm not letting go.

Tick tick tick.

Come on!

And whether the storm or God hears me screaming, the wind gives for a split second and I take it, ripping Eve toward me, caging her in my arms, falling back and smacking the ground hard. The wind's lashing again, pulling us toward the ledge, and I'm digging my nails into rock and Eve's digging her nails into me and together we're digging our nails into hope while time keeps tick tick ticking.

Chapter Twenty-One

I feel the rawness of the air and the tenderness of the light and I hear the birds chirping like they've always chirped and maybe always will. Hours have passed, along with the tornadoes.

I'm rubbing my stinging chest, skin warm and freezing. Eve's clutching my hand and her eyes are opening and closing. We're sitting, slumped. Benjamin's holding Bud secure and peering at the sea. A rocket of laughter fires from his mouth.

You know how I came upon this mountain? he says, wiping tears from his chin. Saul and Reg were stranded on top of another peak further north of here, both shaking like leaves. You should have seen their sorry-assed selves. Reg had just passed his army pilot certificate and they were doing spot searches for other survivors when Reg lost control of his copter. Strong winds. Hail stones. One of the blades snapped, plus a wheel burst on landing, and it was by God's grace they survived at all. I was doing fire outbreak checks when I spotted 'em. Picked them up real quick and beelined it to Snowy. And we thought *that* was a storm.

His laughter ebbs and he grabs some sand, lets it sift through his fingers.

You know Saul's not even a commander? He's just a low-ranking Navy guy they gave authority to until we get rescued.

A pause hangs in the air. Eve's slumped, rubbing her thigh. It's too dark to see much bruising, but I wouldn't be surprised if we were both covered head to toe.

We need to check on the others, I tell her.

Eve's face clouds over. They should be the ones checking on *us*.

I squeeze her hand.

They were panicking. No one thinks straight when they panic.

She looks at me. Well, you're pretty good at it.

Beginner's luck, I say, shrugging.

A strange sound from Bud. I glance over and he's gnawing at his bandage.

Come here, Buddy. Let me help.

Benjamin releases him and he pads over, tail wagging high, oblivious to the cliff edge only feet away, though the difference in weather is something else. The air's motionless and raw peach, tender from the tempest's lashing. The calm after the storm.

Still. I wipe my drenched brow.

We need to get dry and get off this mountain, I say.

Benjamin stretches his legs.

Got that right. Now that the storm's past, Sky Station's signal should be up and running clear again, telling us what's what.

I toss him a look while tugging Bud's bandage off, then look to the sea floating calm and flat and turning black.

Those boats docked in the harbor, I ask Benjamin. They in working order?

Some are. All have been ransacked, though.

And there's a few boatpods, I reckon?

Yep. They'll be working, alright.

My Pa sailed in one once. You?

I wish, he says. Apparently they're even more futuristic than they look. Rumor has it they're loaded with special effects and have more lift than a hovercraft.

I scrape my fingers through the dirt.

Why hasn't anyone sailed off in them?

Power supply's too unpredictable, he says. Though there's another reason.

His fingers fiddle with the gauze around his head.

Tell me. What have you two noticed since you've arrived on this mountain? The obvious, I mean.

I look at him. That women outnumber the men?

No. The more obvious.

Folks are scared?

Terrified. They're afraid of the unknown, and no one likes the unknown even more than the unknown they know already. You put a boatpod in front of anyone in that frame of mind and they turn the other away—especially in this weather. A ship's a much safer bet.

I scratch my cheek. So, you're gonna board the ship?

Damn right, I'm gonna board the ship. Can't wait to get back to bacon and eggs and business as usual.

Jack? Is that you? Eve?

A wisp of a voice floating around the corner, close to the gap. We turn our heads to a small figure walking gingerly toward us. I ease myself up, legs cramping, back stiff.

Joan. Go easy now. The path narrows just there.

She halts. Thank God you're alright, she says, wiping her forehead clear of sweat. Sierra thought you two stayed put in the medical tent, but when you weren't there ... is that there fellow the other pilot?

She squints past us toward Benjamin. He gives her a salute.

All accounted for, he says.

You need to come back now, she says straight. All of you. It's safer by the campsite.

Benjamin snorts. I wouldn't go that far.

He gets up slow and slumps past us toward Joan. The sun's lowering behind the mountain top, providing just enough light to navigate. I help Eve up. Stepping to the boulder, I twist 'round quick and slide my fingers over the slit, feeling for the gun and knife. I grab them and pocket them, then join the others. The five of us move along the cliff's edge slow and steady, my legs pins and needling. Bud's limping a touch but otherwise alright. Eve, on the other hand, is struggling. I'm right behind her and she's taking an age, rubbing her thigh every third step, saying it's not serious when I ask.

When we emerge campsite side, I notice the fire has burned itself out. A lantern is hanging from a tree branch, spotlighting the bunker with its door ajar, a herd of people huddled inside. In the shadowy darkness, the tents are grotesque creatures—torn and flung all over the place. By some act of grace, the medical tent is still erect. Last man standing. We watch on as Sierra emerges from the flap, the fabric torn to shreds, holding a torch and blankets. She spots us after a couple of steps and rushes over.

Where were you?

On the other side of the bunker, Benjamin answers.

I thought you had made it inside the bunker. It was pitch black in there and noisy, too. Couldn't hear or see anyone.

Everyone doing alright? I ask her.

Luckily, yes. And the signal's stronger. We should be hearing news about any other storms, or rescue, soon. We'll clean this campsite mess up in the morning.

She lowers her voice. We need to decide what to do with the body, too.

What body? Benjamin looks at each of us in turn.

No one's told you? Sierra says.

No.

The boy. Bobby. Just before the storm hit. Wolves got to him.

How'd you know it was wolves?

Sierra shrugs.

Must have been. They've been getting closer.

The pilot's eyes grow large.

Knew it would happen. This mountain's getting smaller by the minute.

The nurse's chin drops. I know. Cila wants to bury him, but the smell will attract anything prowling. She just needs some time to come to her senses.

Benjamin sighs. Time is what we don't have.

He starts walking toward the medical tent, rubbing his bandage.

Eve wraps her arms around her waist. Been a bitch of a day, she says, shivering.

Sierra nods, motions toward the tent. The cot beds are free, she says. Clean up, get some shut-eye. There's extra clothes, too. People are either setting up camp in the bunker or in their sleeping bags.

We tread over to the medical tent, finding the cabinets and cupboards at all angles, cups and kits on the floor, broken bottles oozing liquid, one of the beds tipped. Eve tidies the equipment while I mop up the liquid with makeshift cloths before Bud gets the chance to slurp. When the space is cleared, each of us towels off and gets dressed behind the curtains. Clothes are a size too big for us both, but who's complaining?

I offer Eve one of the cots, Benjamin the other, then gather some blankets and bundle them on the ground. Bud snuggles in beside me.

Five minutes later, Benjamin is snoring sound. Eve's lying on the cot beside him, but she's wide awake and rubbing her temples.

Can't sleep, either? I ask.

She raises to her elbows. I think most of me's still falling off that cliff.

Tell me about it.

I dig into my pocket, stand up, and hand her the knife. She mouths a thanks and slips it under her pillow.

I look at her. How did you happen to have a knife on you?

Silence floats between us.

My mother gave it to me, she replies.

Really?

When I was a baby. Look, it may have been someone else, but I'd like to think it was her. It was wrapped at the bottom of the basket I was lying in when my father found me in that apple tree. That's how I got my name.

She pulls the blade out from the pillow and rotates the handle in front of me.

See?

Hard to in the darkness, but I can just about make out an engraving etched deep in the hilt, toward the bottom. Three curly letters.

Father let me have it when I turned twelve.

Her jawline hardens, then softens.

I'll always thank him for that, though I think his sister urged him on. Bethany helped raise me, too. I suppose she knew how much it would mean to have something of my mother. Still, I've often wondered how I ended up with folks so opposite to me. So shut behind closed doors. Church, and otherwise.

It's helped you become more of who you are, I tell her straight. Contrast, and all.

Eve stares at me. Then nods.

I never knew why my mother left me in that tree. I've

reasoned that however she came to hold me inside of her womb, she couldn't hold me outside of it. Anyway, all I know is ... all I know is that there's this carved out bit in me just like there is in that tree. Right here.

She points to her chest. I look her in the eye.

Maybe there's carved out spaces in all people, I say. And between them. And maybe that's okay.

She opens her mouth to say something but instead lies back down on the cot, facing away.

What do you want, Eve? I ask her. What do you have to hang your life on? You must have something.

I don't know, she finally replies. Starting over's about as far as I've got.

Chapter Twenty-Two

I'm lying on the blankets beside Bud, gazing at the moon through the shredded cloth of the tent's entrance. The day had trucked on, uneventful except for everyone recovering from the shock of the tornadoes and Benjamin and Reg firing eyes across the campfire at lunch and dinner and most times in between. It's deep in the night and Eve's been sleeping for a while now.

I move as quiet as I can so as to not wake Bud and settle just outside the flap, watching the golden moon rise above the mountain peak, lifting in a sky filled with stars, satellites stuck between. Sky Station's fully visible, beaming brighter than them all.

Sighing heavy into the dark air, I close my eyelids and listen to the water lapping, suddenly realizing I'm hungry for it—for its tugging and tiding and calling me forth.

I stand up stiff and peer toward the bunker. Most folks are sleeping, a few are tossing and turning, fewer still chatting in hushed tones in sleeping bags set close to the campfire. I walk toward the boulders, the moon and the stars guiding me.

Moving through the gap, I see a liquid earth, a dark syrup swaying, maple amber.

I'm looking at the sea and it's looking at me and it's calling. A sea breathing and gently rippling.

Unfurling.

And the feeling gets stronger. Stranger. The ache to leap off this ledge and dive in and float away. Unnerving, but familiar. Unnerving because it's familiar. I lean back against the rock face, back from the pull of the water and I realize something: the sea's always been in me, stirring all this time.

And maybe in Pa all his time.

I gaze up to the Ship in the Sky. Reminds me of the spinning top Pa passed down to me from his Pa. Funny how something so archaic as a spinning top can turn into something so futuristic. The two main lights—positioned at the top and bottom—are beaming vibrant. From viewing close-up pictures in school, there's a dome at the bottom, acting as a viewing deck, keeping watch on everything below and around. Rectangular windows wrap around the Station's waist, and there's a spire perched on top, double the height of the dome below—where central control's situated. Like a church spire, reaching to higher gods. The general sheen, green-blue, appears almost phosphorescent at nighttime, which is right now. A shiver runs through my whole body. I stare for long moments at the living creature floating in a deep, dark ocean.

Friend or foe, I don't know.

My breath catches as I stand up and turn 'round.

Slowly, I tread past the boulders and return to Eve and Bud and Benjamin.

All three are still sleeping.

So I stay waking.

I stay waking.

Chapter Twenty-Three

At least a quarter of an hour has passed since I woke up from a shaky sleep and found Bud gone. I've circled the campsite twice, maybe three times. I'm exhausted but pumped with panic. Everyone's sleeping so I can't shout out his name, though I want to scream it as loud as I can. I rush back to the medical tent, shoulders dropping at the sight of his small impression left in the blankets. Grabbing a torch off the cabinet, I make my way past the bunker toward the lantern hanging on the pine tree, then past it toward more pines where his paw prints are stamping the soil. I turn left onto the nearest path leading up the peak.

My dog's sheepish but not stupid. He wouldn't go searching through dense bush or anywhere risky. His nose would have picked up human scent and gone with it.

Fifty steps up the track and I halt. There's howling in the far distance. I keep stepping, my lungs tight, the air cramped.

Bud? Hey, Bud, it's me.

Noiseless now, except the breeze ruffling the needles. After that onslaught of wind and sea spray, the smell of pine is pungent.

I click the flashlight and wave it across the trees and bushes. Bugs dart and wheel in the shock of light and a small creature scatters into a hole just shy of the path. I continue up the meandering incline, grateful for its gradual slope, calling to Bud, louder.

A whooshing sound feet away. I flick the torch and another creature scatters. Skinny mole, or fat rat. I continue climbing, ears pricked for larger things movin', fiercer things howlin'. I turn a bend and the sea comes into clearer view. Stars are spreading over a curve of pre-dawn sky—black tinted with violet. Never climbed high enough to see that curve before. A single star, big and bright, is bobbing on the horizon, about to sink into the sea. I walk on.

Maybe I've gone up the wrong path. Maybe Bud's somehow tucked himself in that same boulder that housed the knife and gun, having found a different gap leading, our paths somehow crossing.

I climb for another quarter-hour until the track leads to a cave of sorts—a large chunk bitten out of a huge rock. I trudge over and slump onto the ledge, arms clasping my legs, head tucked between, taking stock.

I don't even know what day it is.

My arms clasp firmer.

Soft whimpering behind me. I jerk 'round. Bud is hunkered down at the back of the rock. A shadow of a shadow, a crumpled outline.

Grabbing my torch, I flick the switch and angle the beam at his paws so as not to scare him. The light grazes the stone floor. Bud's wagging slight, though he's staring right past me, eyes locked. I spin, expecting a wolf or the whole pack. Instead, it's Reg, standing twenty feet from me, rigid. I raise the torch to his face. The bridge of his nose has been stitched with a two-inch suture. He squints.

Lower that thing, will ya?

I drop the beam to his chest.

It's time for you to go, farm boy. I don't want you in my camp no more.

I angle the flashlight to his waist. He's gripping a wrench.

Can't do what you're askin', I tell him. I need to go back to the camp. For whenever rescue comes.

He spits a wad of tobacco on the ground, points to that bobbing, sinking star just visible through the trees.

Have you looked at the ocean lately? That light out there, that's our ship coming. Real soon. But you're not gonna be on it, because I don't want you on it.

He steps closer. Bud stays back. I stay put.

I need to get on that ship, I tell him. So does Eve.

Eve's not your problem anymore.

He raises the wrench. Motions to the path.

Let me make myself real clear here. If you go back to the camp, I'm gonna kill you. The choice is yours. The track's right there. Take your dog. Take yourself. It's time for you to go.

I stare him in the eye.

Can't do that.

He cocks his head, rolls the tobacco around on his tongue. Drops the wrench on the ground and reaches for something in his back pocket.

Hey, pooch, look what I got more of.

Reg unravels a slab of meat from a plastic wrapper. It's dripping with juice. Bud pads forwards, tongue draping.

Bud. Stop.

He doesn't.

Bud. Come!

Bud scuttles over to the ledge and grabs the meat. Reg scoops him up in his arms.

Attaboy.

My insides turn.

You've got plenty of women to choose from, I tell him.

I want her.

I bite my tongue.

She can make up her own mind.

Reg chuckles foul.

Well, the way I view it is like this. You got two options. You take your loyal doggy friend here and hit the road right now, or you hit the road alone.

He crooks his arm around Bud's neck. What's left of the meat drops out of Bud's mouth and falls to the soil.

I take a step toward. Reg snarls.

What, you gonna use your fist again?

Put my dog down.

What's it gonna be, farm boy?

I reach for my back pocket. Pull out the gun. Reg freezes.

Bet that thing doesn't even have bullets, he says slow.

Put Bud down.

Sure thing.

In one shift motion, Reg lowers to one knee and slams Bud onto his side. Bud yelps and squirms, but gets nowhere. His tongue's starting to bulge.

I may not have believed in it before—the Devil— but now I do. Reg starts twisting. He starts twisting Bud's neck while I start shouting. Time stops then, in no time at all. In Reg's eyes, I'm seeing every disaster there ever was, and in Bud's, whatever love's left over, and an earthquake comes rumbling so quick, I'm shaking panic-mad, but my hand's holding the gun and my arm's holding my hand and my heart's holding onto the only world I got left, so I click, aim, fire, then all goes hush.

All except the pounding in my ears.

I hold my eyelids shut. Can't look. Have to. When I do, times starts rushing ahead and the pounding's on the outside—Bud's thumping toward me with a shock of plum splattered over his coat. I gaze down at my gun.

I've just shot a man.

I squint at Reg's lame body bent double on the ground three yards yonder, blood pouring from his head. Hearing nothing save for birds squawking, Bud and I bolt it down the mountain.

Chapter Twenty-Four

There's blood on Bud, and now there's blood on me. I try sprinting without tumbling, leading Bud without tripping. Twigs are cracking underfoot. Shapes are looming close, far, then close again. Every time I glance back, I'm sure Reg is following—shadows and sounds are doing scary things between the dappled starlight and the breeze. Sharp edges and imaginings. Ghosts of what's past and maybe what's to come.

When I reach base camp, I'm clear out of breath, though wired with adrenalin and alarm. I've been so busy bolting, I force myself to halt and duck out of sight just in time behind one of the pine trees as a young woman hustles past, looking for something.

Over here, someone shouts.

The woman turns on her heels and leaves me clamping Bud's muzzle shut.

Quit whining, I whisper.

Still clamping till I realize I'm squeezing his ribs like a vice. I loosen my hold and survey the surrounds. Another fire's going, plumes of smoke rising. The smell is acrid, noxious. Folks are feeding it all kinds of things—broken poles, bits of fabric, strips of wood. Dawn's arrived and brushing thin streaks of light across the campsite, and people are making the most of it, packing and clearing up.

I hear scratches of conversation. Snippets about signals and ships and timing and weather. The atmosphere is more edgy than elevated. I sweep my eyes to the ocean and can't see for the trees, but I imagine the vessel's getting closer inch by inch, a floating city on a slippery sea.

I take a step forward and the medical tent comes into view, its tattered flap tied back by a ribbon, with Eve standing right in front. Can't see her expression, but her arms are crossed firm. After standing like that for minutes, she tucks herself back into the tent. She's the only shadow moving inside. Now's my chance.

I pick Bud up and tiptoe past the pine tree, giving its lantern a wide berth, then head 'round the front of the bunker, straightening up when I get to the bushes. My arms graze thorns as I pass. Some folks are poking around the depths of the bunker. I make a quick calculation of where the opened hatch is and where I'll be sprinting past. Anyone looking toward the entrance will see us as clear as day.

Shit. Someone is looking toward the entrance: Joan. But I've got no other options, so I make a cross in her direction and fly past anyway.

Oh. My. God.

Eve's jaw drops open.

Shhhh.

I place a finger to my mouth and motion to the water bucket positioned on the other side of the tent. She nods, eyes flitting to Bud's coat. I plop him in the corner while she rushes outside. I tell Bud to sit still, then grab some cloths and a grungy towel hanging from a hook, rip my rain jacket and shirt off.

Eve comes back with the bucket, arms stretched long. I hurry over and take the handles.

What happened? she asks.

You know the ship's coming, right?

Yeah. But—

Well, I'm not going to be on it. You can either get on it, or you can come with me. Your call.

Fuck. I sound like Reg. But there's no time to be courteous.

She stares at me wide-eyed. I place my hands on her shoulders.

You got one minute to decide.

Someone's outside. I turn, frantic, scrubbing my jacket, my shirt. I slap some water over Bud's coat. That someone's coming closer. Coming inside.

I jerk 'round.

Give me the gun.

Benjamin's standing next to Eve, taking in Bud's pink fur and my red-speckled chest. He holds out his palm.

Give me the gun, he repeats.

Christ, Benjamin. I don't have time for this.

Damn right, you don't.

He steps forward. We lock eyes.

I'm not handing it over.

How many bullets left?

One.

He rubs his jaw. What happened?

Reg happened. Okay?

Dead, happened?

I glance at Eve. She's shaking. Taking the whole of me in.

You coming? I ask her.

Eve closes her eyelids. Opens them.

I thought you were more the saving than the killing kind, *Jack*.

I look at Bud, then back at her, squinting harsh. Your call. I'm heading to the boatpods soon as I get a gap.

Benjamin steps backwards, coughing into his palm.

Listen, he says. There's a drop from the edge of the helicopter landing pad straight down to the main dock. Take the path that we took up, then turn right at the landing pad. The terrain's rough, but it's the short cut you'll need before folks start heading down. Saul's waiting on Reg to return from his trek up the mountain. Told Saul he was going to a higher elevation to check on the ship's distance.

I swallow hard.

A voice blaring. Male. Rough.

He's calling for Benjamin. The pilot looks at me, about to say something, but then a wave of footfall tumbles toward the tent. Benjamin lurches.

Play couple, he whispers.

He presses Eve up against me as Saul barges in. I wrap my arms around her, then glance over her shoulder like I'm startled at seeing both men here.

Found 'em, Benjamin says with a grin.

Eve keeps her trembling hands on my chest, covering the stains. Benjamin steps in front of Bud. Saul grunts something, stares us down.

You seen Reg?

No.

You sure about that?

Yes.

He turns to Benjamin. I'm going to circle the campsite again, then head up the mountain. The smoke should keep the wolves at bay, but I'm getting worried for Reg. He should have been back by now. Until I return, you're in charge of getting these people down the mountain. Plus, Bobby's mother is adamant to bury her boy. Gather some men to do it quick.

I've got it from here, Benjamin says solemn. Any more news about the ship?

Saul licks his bottom lip. It's docking in under an hour.

Chapter Twenty-Five

Inch by inch, the vessel is sailing toward us. The crowd's looking on, standing right at the cliff's edge, some leaning slightly over as though they could reach out and tug it closer.

It's near enough to see it's a container ship, not a cruise liner. Towers are stacked next to each other: brown and rust and wine. Small and tall and fat. I guess Sky Station was trying to lighten things up by calling it a "holiday vessel."

Eve and I are standing behind the others, Bud at my feet. The harbor is out of sight, but I know it'll be lit by the peeking sun soon. Eve is watching me watching the sea. A pearly glow is angling over this side of the mountain, striking the distant ship's hull just so, making it glint.

The crowd is beginning to disperse, rapid chatterings about having to pack up in a hurry. Damnit that I didn't get away before the crowd blocked the path leading to the helicopter pad. Saul was pacing back and forth across the campsite for a while, circling the medical tent like he knew I was gonna flee.

Eve and I hang back. I tug on her sleeve and whisper in her ear, antsy.

I gotta go. Now.

She glances toward the ship. You sure you want to risk leaving all by yourself?

My lungs squeeze. The ship's approaching from the south side of Brown Mountain, far enough away to sail away without being spotted if I make a run for it. I'll head north first, then angle east.

My body's tense, expecting Saul to come charging at any moment. I spot Joan and Sierra trailing behind everyone. Joan turns abrupt and squints at Eve and I and Bud.

You coming? she asks.

Eve throws me a look. Tears are welling.

Yeah, is all she says.

Joan hesitates, nods, then turns and walks on. Eve's staring at me. She opens her mouth, closes it, turns away. If only I had the time to explain. A moment of dead silence, and I watch her walk away from me. I watch her go.

Sighing heavy, I wait till her steps grow faint, then start running in the opposite direction, fast, Bud trailing close.

Take care of yourself, Jack.

I spin around. It's Benjamin, jogging to me, catching his breath.

You too, I say. Look, I gotta go. Can't talk—

I know. You've a clue where you're heading?

I glance at the horizon.

I figure there's only one sea and it only goes in one direction.

And which direction would that be?

Whichever one you want it to go in.

He chuckles soft. Well, maybe I'll see you on the other side of that.

He tilts his head to the path behind us.

Don't worry about Eve. Saul won't get past me, you hear?

I give him what passes for a smile, then a thumbs up. He smiles, lifts his thumb, then motions me and Bud on. We descend swiftly, the crisp mountain air shifting to sour-sweet sea, bronze soil turning sand. Layers of gold and sapphire are unrolling along the morning horizon. I'm feelin' dizzy, but it's just the thrill of touching the sea that's coursin' through me. I've heard the salt makes you float and cuts right through and tastes like seaweed, too.

Three-quarters way down the path and what's left of the harbor comes into view—the boats docked and chattering in the welcoming waves. The container ship is slinking further 'round Brown, a coppery flame.

I sight the ramp in the distance, rickety and sway-ing. Most of the sailboats have been swept clear of sails, ropes, lifejackets. The boatpods are docked fur-thest away, more compact and capsule-shaped with clear domes roofs. Dirty footprints running all over. Bud pads ahead, sniffing and wagging, stopping just short of the ramp when he sees it moving. I collect him in my arms and guide us across, then down another ramp to a smaller dock, waterlogged and already smoothing out from the saltwater kissing it all the while. I look back at the mountain. No one's charging, and no one's following, neither.

I walk tentative across the soggy dock toward the first boatpod, a twenty-footer, still intact. I'd be more amazed seeing this beauty in the flesh if my heart wasn't in my mouth. Apple wood interior. Fiberglass exterior. Oval deck surrounding. Solar panels and unbreakable mast. Born to last.

I check for the ship, and it's breaking clear past Brown. I inhale sharp and lower Bud onto the deck. It creaks and tilts as the boom strap slides back and forth, slapping. The helm is sterling and solid. I touch the wheel and my dog looks on, curious.

For when you want to use your own hands, I tell him.

Praying for luck, I open the hatch and leap into the cabin, search the control board, and flick what looks to be the power cell. It comes alive, blinking bright red. I breathe relief. There's an emergency button with options for limited signal strength. I make it simple and choose Auto-Sail, due north. Then I check the stores fast as I can. No food, no water, but there's a silicon-type box with a guidebook on how to turn saltwater into drinkable water, plus a rain jacket and small-scale fishing rod hidden under one of the seats.

Wait here, I instruct Bud.

I climb out and jump onto the other boatpod. Seeing even less on offer, I rush back empty-handed, press the activation button on the control board, unknot the ropes tying boat to dock, then sit on the stern, my dog held snug between my knees. He keeps sniffing the air, looking this way and that, but he's otherwise placid. I stay mute, clutching the rigging joints, listening to the boat release its anchor and start its engine, the wind whistling across the cinches. Then the boat pulls away.

Then it doesn't. I scour the hull, the engine revving restless. Damnit. There's one more rope near the stern still attached. I launch myself at the knot but my fingers find no purchase. Scrambling down to the cabin, the engine sputtering, I'm about to click the switch off when—through the glass dome—something silver flashes. Silver mixed with bone.

I leap up the steps. Do a double take.

Eve's sawing her knife through the fraying cord, flaxen hair flaying about. Bud's grinning and licking her knees.

The rope snaps clean. I pull her toward me as the boatpod lurches forward, her blade barely missing my chest. I inhale, she exhales, and the auto-pilot steers us out of the harbor as fast as it can, the waves rocking us in their tide like rock-a-bye baby. Like the song Ma used to sing when I was small and sleeping. Something catches in my throat.

Eve's standing right beside me, shaking as much as I am. I reach for her hand.

You okay?

She places her trembling palm in mine, then leans against my body. Waits a moment, then speaks.

Joan made me change my mind.

I wipe beads of sweat from my forehead.

She took me aside just after you fled, while her and I were walking on the path back to the campsite. Said she had a strong sense that I should meet you on your path, too. For us to journey together. Spoke of how God's always gives people a second chance, maybe more.

I grin.

I'll explain, I say. Just let's get a little further out to sea. Gotta leave those ghosts behind me for a minute.

She shifts her feet, nods, then glances at the ship and the mountain, both growing smaller by the second.

Think Joan will be alright? Think we will? What you said about Sky Station keeping information from us—

She cuts off, eyes as wide as a child's.

I don't know about the Ship in the Sky, I tell her straight, but Joan's got God and I've got a gun. And no one fucks with either.

She laughs. A freeing laugh, soaring right across the ocean. She flares me a smile, then asks if the boat-pod's got means for connection with Sky Station.

Haven't even thought to check.

I'll check the cabin and see what's what, she says, standing up straight and stepping past me. My skin's still tingling from her touch.

Another moment and my mind's wandering to Ma and Pa. Bill and Betty. Tommy. Frank. Then to school friends and school bullies. Haven't thought of any of them much over the last few days. I wonder who's made it. Thinking those who didn't might be better off.

I pad toward Bud. He's peering over the bow, at all the life circling in the deep. I steady my hand on his back, pull off my boots, and dip my toes in the clear water, its ebbing and flowing as natural as breath. Then I ruffle his coat as he licks my toes and tell him we're leaving and arriving. That it's time to stop, and time to move on.

He cocks his head at me.

You know something, Buddy? Some say you find your tribe. Others say your tribe finds you. And maybe it can be both. But however much folks travel together, the truth is each man is a tribe within himself, true and solid.

We sit side by side, him looking down and me looking forward.

Taking one last look at the mountain and seeing no one and hearing nothing, I return to the stern and untether from all I used to believe in. From all I was forced to be.

Then I take the helm.

Elle Evans is a Transpersonal Psychotherapist and author. She is Welsh, though having moved so many times, her accent is decidedly mid-Atlantic. Elle is penning three novels on the go, one of which is the next installment following *Ship in the Sky* in the Earthlight series. She lives in Cape Town, South Africa.